Glitter, Blood & Tears

Ryan Mathew Schulz

DEDICATION

This book is dedicated to John Curtin College of the Arts, Fremantle
Western Australia. The *real* Lumiere College of the Arts. This dedication
goes out to the College and the teachers which I had connectivity with
between 2002 – 2006. Those who supported me throughout my senior
school years will never be forgot.

Thanks specifically to;
(Alphabetically)

Ms Beringer
Ms Bishop
Ms Ivicevic

Thanks for not casting me aside when things got tough, allowing me to
continue my studies at the college with my peers, and providing me with the
foundation of support that I needed in difficult times.

CONTENTS

FOREWORD

Eight years ago I took it upon myself to pursue the career of a drag queen. After coming runner up in an annual drag extravaganza within my first year, I was later selected to represent Western Australia in a national competition as Miss WA. Part of my journey lead me to produced a theatre production entitle 'DRAG' which explored the motivations, inspirations and creations of "the man underneath the wig", throwing back as far as Shakespearian times when men played female roles.

I must thank Mr. John Aitken for the research and time that he invested in 'DRAG' to help bring my vision to life, and Louise Coles for her constant belief in me at that time, her continuous support and ongoing encouragement, which was paramount in achieving what I have and what I'm sure I will. I must also thank my partner Blake, for his incredible backing in all my previous pursuits, and for always managing to give me a boost in reassurance for whatever situation I find myself in – you truly are my rock. A large thank you which might be thought to go without saying - but even in this progressive world both many gay and bisexual men still receive both metaphorical and physical kicks in the gut from those whom you'd think would be the ones to support them - and as such my big thanks goes to my parents Donna and Neville, who have never failed to show their confidence and pride in me, and provided the guidance and never ending love that's never gone unnoticed.

I have recently retired from the world of drag, looking to pursue other aspects of performance art and creative fields. This book is my tribute to the elapsed part of my life that was *Panache*, and while 'Glitter, Blood & Tears' is not based on a true story, it certainly takes part in sharing many insights of the motions which I and others in my life have gone through… complete with a little graphic imaginational creation for your sick pleasure.

Ryan Michael Schulz
December 2015

1 THE CONCEPTUALISATION

Here I am. Sat at my dressing table, surrounded by a large
assortment of costumes I've collected over a multitude of years. Each of
them made from various fabrics and hung according to colour. Purples,
pinks, blues, greens, yellows, sequins, velvets, crushed-velvets, satins, you
name it. More costumes than I've had a need for, really. Fixed to the walls
of the room in which I'm sat, are shelves with rows of my favourite wigs.
Blondes, brunettes and two-toned beauties. Straight wigs, curly wigs, wavy
wigs, full wigs, teased wigs, short wigs and long wigs. Just to name a few.
The drawers to my right are filled with costume jewellery, fake eyelashes,
half-used tubs of eyebrow wax and imitation stick on finger nails. The
drawers to my left hold a selection of foundations in various shades for
contouring, a multitude of eye-shadows for prettifying and a collection of
some rather useless crap. Crap like cheap imported strips of crystals, which
would have fallen to bits when I originally opened them I'm sure. Things

like that stay left where they fall of late. Sure when you first get into the bizz its fun, exciting and almost enjoyable to arrange and maintain a room full of campery. But somewhere down the line the arrangement, upkeep and pride of ones assets seems to become mundane and banal.

The room is filled with scents of musk and powder, with the faint aroma of overworn unwashed materials and a hint of body odor. To the trained and seeking eye, one could sight the odd stain of sweat on my costumes' joins at the underarm. However, to those blinded by the end of a week's hard work, seeking entertainment and enrichment in their lives, wishing to escape reality for a night of music and performance, these costumes have brought many a smile to many a face, and many a show the glistening of a hundred captured sequins met with the eye of the spotlight.

Here I still sit, on a chair covered in makeup smudges. I look down to the surface of my dresser, covered by a light layer of set translucent powders and home to small mementoes which are placed in hope of inspiring and motivating me again one day. One memento I've held dearly, is a framed picture of a guest star I once had the pleasure of performing alongside. Complete with her signature it reads *Sacrifice, You fierce bitch! Love Inga xxx* Inga Ingénue of the Atomic Bombshells was her name, a performer from Seattle. Being the capital of 'drag', Seattle is a place of which I used to aspire to go one day, to see the true art form in all its glory.

Though Inga herself, unlike me, was one hundred per cent female born and bred, yet still she considered what she did to be 'drag'. Although her acts were burlesque by definition. Loud, vivacious and flirtatious, Inga was so beautiful, tasteful, sensual and arousing all at the same time. Her body built to please all men, women and those that identified otherwise or sat in-between. Breasts so supple, a body so smooth, with a face only to be described as that of a goddess. She had plump lips, glistening green eyes and a complexion which Miss World herself would die for. Men swooned over her, and women stared in admiration. Yet, even with her picture, signed in front of me, the seductress herself could not put a spark back into my love for what I once had such a passion for.

Here I'm still sat, now looking into my eyes through the mirror of the dresser in front of me. It has seen so many of my faces. It has seen moments of fear, sadness and regret, yet also joy and happiness. Endless faces full of endless emotions. Just now, a tear trickles out from one of my eyes, making its way down my cheek to where it holds itself at the bottom of my jaw. I wonder if I should let it drop or wipe it before it gets the chance. Before having the option to decide, another tear forms and follows. Observing them emotionlessly, the force of gravity pulls the two tears together, and down to join the surface of set translucent powder. I close my eyes and take a deep breath in through my nostrils. Exhaling, I open my eyes, again looking into them through the mirror. *What is this all for?* I think to myself. The exhaustion of it all. The investment in time and energy. The constant repetition that has become this heightened and uplifted yet in-genuine persona, complete with impersonal conversations and social interactions. The sheer and continuous battle with today's modern culture of tall poppy syndrome. Every miserable beings ability to drag anyone who's thriving in the world a minuet bit more than them, down to their level of pathetic worth. My ulter ego, *Sacrifice*, had quite literally become a sacrifice for what has now become my life. But, the show must go on. I muster up some strength and will to open the top drawer of my dresser and scavenge for some eye liner. I find an old shortened down and pre-sharpened one. I remember when it was once full, strong and clean from grubby finger marks of muck. I start to apply a line of black to my lower eyelid. I pause with a slight quiver to my hand. I look deep into my eyes in the mirror. I imagine a flicker of blood, a knife clenched tight in my fist, and the slit of a throat.

Back to reality. I had slashed a black line of eyeliner across the mirror. I let out a scream, flexing my hands and bringing my palms towards my forehead. Is it so wrong for me to imagine? To imagine getting into my car tonight, with a knife from the kitchen nestled into my costume bag. To rock up to the venue I perform at, where I'm never challenged to show security inside my bag because I'm considered royalty. Where I can walk right through the doors off the streets into a club, filled with bright flashing lights, colour and music, into a room where I'm greeted with smiles and waved at by a flock of adoring punters. To a place where every week I'm offered drinks on arrival and known to the bar staff by name. Is it wrong to imagine walking through the crowd of people dancing, on to the stage and through to the dressing room door, bursting my way through, taking out my kitchen knife to start slitting the throats of every drag queen I see? I imagine starting with *Miss Ima No'mans*. When I get there tonight she'll most probably be in the dressing room at the counter, touching up her mascara, ignoring anyone that enters or comes her way like the arrogant person she is. Filled with ego and attitude, her head is honestly shoved so far up her arse that I wouldn't even have to use a knife to kill the bitch, I'd just pull her body and her neck would snap clean off. Leaving her head to sniff her own shit for all eternity. I'd honestly walk in, and she wouldn't even so much as batter an eyelash my way. She wouldn't acknowledge my presence in any form whatsoever.

It would be easy you know, to walk right up behind her while she's busy maintaining her arrogant persona, that by the time she'd finished applying her mascara, I'd have pulled out my knife and done what needed to be done. She wouldn't even flinch. Wrapped up in her own world, Ima

No'mans is the queen which all queens don't dare cross. Sucked up to by all, yet her attitude and antics are gossiped about by all. Considering herself No'mans 'the vision', she struts through the club like there ain't no body in sight. Bump into her and spill *your own* drink, you better buy *her* one. An attitude to behold, but even more so her figure. As all mighty as she portrays herself, No'man's body is something which must be beheld onto itself. A fat lump, pushed and manipulated by her corset to get an hourglass shape which features large thighs and back fat, conveniently covered by the dark shadows of the nightlife. As I'd slit her throat, I imagine thick masses of fat as thick as her attitude bursting out from her neck. A cake-faced lot of lard at most, yet no-one dare defies her. An intriguing operation of what is called 'the scene'.

Made up of a few characters, the scene is rather something, consumed by alcohol, sex and drugs. There is what's known as the plastics, the ones who compact as much makeup and bronzer onto their faces as a corpse at its wake. They most often wear short shorts and loose fitted singlets, with bleach blonde hair and usually lip gloss to fin. Prancing about and walking through the club like they're America's next top model, they accept no hook-up but from one of their own. Although, potential makeovers, are often considered. The plastics are often mistaken as twinks, but twinks do classify as their own. Almost always new to the scene, twinks are young, thin and out for a dance. Inexperienced, easily manipulated, none the wiser and ready to jump when the first person that gives them attention in the club says to do so. Then there are your bears and cubs, men who may have very well have once been plastics or twinks, but have gained some love handles and let their body hair run wild – plastics and twinks often waxing and shaving the sight of any hair from their skin. Don't get me wrong, bears might groom, but they very much keep their chests hairy and faces full-breaded. And leather - let's not forget the leather. They *love* to be seen out in their leather vests, caps, hats, pants, shorts, shirts, jock-straps or braces. Of course there are others, as well as your average gays that don't quite fit into a box, or as some call them 'passing gays'. The ones that could pass for straight, if they liked. Often with their own group of friends before conforming to others expectations – like the divide of groups in high school. I never did get the creation of minorities within a minority, but that's just how it is. Nevertheless, your average gay just heads out with old friends from school, work colleagues, and can sometimes be caught dragging their own mother out for a dance. Unlike the plastics, who wouldn't dream of such a thing. Let's not forget the fag hags, girls who hang around the gays like a lingering bad smell, considering them their best friends, over-exaggerating everything while screaming at the top of their lungs. These girls are almost usually always found with a bottle of vodka in one hand and a cigarette in the other. More often than not, a society-norm misfit themselves, oh boy do them fag hags love to push their way into the lives of us gays. Oh, and let's not forget the lesbians. The butch ones often mistakenly hit on by us gays, seemingly male from behind or at a side glance. There's the lipsticks too – not to be mistaken as a fag hag – they're loud, clingy and often make up for their low self-esteem by caking on as much foundation and lippy as a drag queen. Which of course, finally, there are the drag queens. The ones who think they rule and own the scene, always self-promoting, taking selfies, competing, and oh the judgmental bitching. Never be fooled by the stunning looks that these queens showcase. No sooner that an admiring patron at the club is complimenting a queens attire and walking away with a selfie, is that very queen turning as quick as quick can be with some snarky remark to their flock on the persons fowl teeth, frizzy hair or un-styled attire. Not that you'd ever know it through the endearing smile which majority of the queens master in plastering on their face when approached.

After ridding of No'mans, the next beauty in my plan of attack would be *Angelica Absolute*, the head queen of the club and two-faced cat who upfront seems polite and welcoming, but behind one's back holds a knife ready for when you turn the other way. Absolute holds the reigns in beauty and fierce looks of the scene. From glowing fluorescent outfits with mohawks and piercings, to long glowing gowns with trains of glitter which fall behind her as she floats her way down the stage. Hair sprayed to a tee with not one strand of hair loose, she takes all the glory when it comes to any success of the club. In fact she's been known to take the glory for the firing of staff she hasn't even bothered to say hello to. Despite the club being run by a small management team, Absolute takes the credit, and nobody dares confront her if other truths were brought to light. Upon slitting No'man's throat, I'd drag her body behind the black curtains which line the dressing room, taking her seat while using her blood as a lipstick. Absolute would enter to see me touching up my face, and approach me from behind, placing her hands on my shoulders.

"All set?" she'd ask.

I'd turn myself around to face her. Then, standing up, with my knife conveniently tucked into the side of my corset, I'd proceed to answer her.

"Feeling better than ever," I'd say, "in for a killer of a night". No doubt she'd sense my tone of angst and ask if everything was okay. I picture spinning in the chair and looking up to the ceiling crazily to unsettle her. "I'm just fine," I'd answer, "but I think the person you should be asking is No'mans... although perhaps before I slit her throat" I'd finish, laughing in hysterics while traces of blood leaked from my lips onto my teeth.

The music in the club would be so loud, with no one able to hear

Absolute as she cries out for help. I'd jump ahead one step faster than her. Prepared, while she had no idea what was to come. Leaping to the door and locking it, I'd approach her slowly as she asked what she could do to help me. I'd simply approach and answer her with the response, *to die*. Hacking at her chest, I can only at this stage anticipate the feelings of adrenaline, triumph and fulfilment that I'd indulge in. Her blood would surely make its way onto my face with each jab at chest. But what's more, I'd want to smear it while it was still warm. Leaving her body for the club queens to find, I'd unlock the door, keep it ajar, and move to the corner of the room once detaching the handle. Upon their arrival, at first they'd stumble in as a group, a little bandwagon of queens, laughing and waving their hands about. The first to notice would point out the body after the others made their way in and shut the door, now with no handle to escape. The first one to run and kneel to see if the body was okay would be the last to leave. Vulnerably situated on the floor, she'd most probably try to get up in a panic as I started hacking into others around her, in turn twisting or spraining an ankle as her heels gave way.

Upon walking into the room, as their focus became engrossed with what was going on, I'd initially start with the most separated from the group, more reserved than the others. I'd place my arm around the queen closest to the back of the room, as if to hold her in comfort, then drive my knife into her neck up to her jaw. Yanking the knife out and allowing her body to fall to the floor as she held her neck with gushing blood, the room would start to distress and the queens will try to fight back. But I know I'd win. Those fuckers would have it coming, waving their hands around like little pansies. I'd slice and dice into every last pretty little cake-faced one of them, making sure not even their parents could identify them. For a moment I'd indulge in my accomplishment. I'd gather the blood from their bodies spilled out onto the floor, and smother it over my face like warm water after cleansing. I'd smell the sweet fragrance of victory and justice, and as I look at the room of ugliness put to rest around me, I'd let go of the knife, re-attach the door handle and make my way out onto the stage. Here, I'd receive my true moment of appreciation. A moment of recognition. Here, I will go down in history.

I will walk in front of the DJ booth where the lights should direct once the tech gets wind of a drag performer on stage. Unsure of what I am doing, presuming I was about to announce the next feature of the night, the music would fade out. I will stand, head held high, while the image of a blood-soaked drag queen imprints into the minds of all the club's punters. Making sure I'd worn my sleekest glove-fitting sequin dress, it will hang heavy to the floor with blood as it sparkles in the spotlight. Surely someone will go backstage into the dressing room to see what the meaning of the whole situation is. And to that person's horrific surprise, there will be nothing inside but lifeless bodies. It may take a while for people to realise what has happened or what is going on, but once that person backstage re-emerges and screams *murderer*, mayhem will break loose. I will smile in my magnificence, before they take me away, taking my bow on stage, one last time.

Back to reality, I begin to wonder if I am conceptualising something. If I'd conceptualized exactly as it will go down. My body starts to fill with exhilaration, determination and excitement. I even crack a smirk as I continue to stare at myself in the mirror. Is it these thoughts that have kept me going? Was it the imagining or conceptualising of such events that has kept me from giving up? Although these thoughts entered my mind, never once have I gone to the extent of putting a knife in my bag. Never once. If I did do it though, and I went through with this, how would it go down once I was taken away? No doubt the media would take hold of it. Headlines along the lines of, *Drag queen massacre: The highest heels left standing.* Could I plead insanity? Maybe I actually am insane? Do other people think like this? I'm not sure. But in the big scheme of things, what's wrong and right after all? As humans we've laid down laws, laws that weren't among us when the first humans walked the earth. Even so, before that, I doubt the dinosaurs trampled the world second-thinking before they conquered their next nemesis or prey. I'm sure many a dinosaur battled with only one left standing, not thinking twice if what it did was right or wrong. It would be pure survival. Even today, lions, crocodiles, tigers, cheetahs and other animals are out for the kill. Out to survive. Humans only obey the law because they were brought up to do so. Not even all humans at that. In putting all I've learnt to rest and listening to my inner self, what do I think is the right thing to do? How do *I* survive? To others it will seem cruel and barbaric, but again, in a world with created laws, rules and morals it's just how they were raised, right? Who's to say the people we have been raised by are the ones that are right? Who's to say that the people that laid the laws down before them were too? To my mind, there should be exceptions. To my mind, this is one.

On the outside listening in on my thoughts, people may be shocked, appalled, disgusted or somewhat concerned. But, by god, if they only knew. These queens are evil. Pure evil. Have we not been brought up in a society where we've learn that evil must be stopped? Countless stories spring to mind. Whether it be fiction or non-fiction, Godzilla or Adolf Hitler, are we not accustomed to react? To do something about it? In a 1980's film entitled *The Dead Zone*, a man named Johnny Smith played by actor Christopher Walken is given the power of sight – which they call the dead zone – enabling him to see into the future. This sight presents Johnny with the ultimate choice of whether to take the opportunity to kill a man who he knows will destroy the world. In fact, he asks the question 'if you could go back in time to Germany, before Hitler came to power, knowing what you know now, would you kill him?' If I could end the pain and agony tonight for all, wouldn't I be doing something for the greater good? If I took this step tonight, I could prevent a lifetime of torment for many.

2 CHILDHOOD

Looking down from my seat, I release my right hand from a clenched grip which had formed around my eyeliner. Confused for a minute as I thought I had dropped it. As I release the tension in my hand, I realise that I have pierced my palm. It begins to trickle with blood. The mere thought of these scene queens had my body in physical distress. I wondered if I had ever felt like this before, and if other people ever had such an effect on me. Was I being logical like Christopher Walken, or was I just plain crazy? Had I just let them get to me? *No, I refuse to believe I'm crazy.*

I recall moments. As a child I grew up like most - at least I presume I did. I had an upbringing from a loving mother and father in the suburbs of Perth, Western Australia. Lived my whole life here. But boy oh boy had I once dreamed to travel the world. Not just Seattle, but New York, Paris and ye old London Town! My dad was in the army, and my mother was an education assistant. My dad travelled a lot, and unfortunately missed out on a lot of my life events. I remember late nights and sometimes early mornings waking up to howling cries from mum. I'd be lying in bed and lift the covers to my nose, looking out into the darkness of my room, unsure of what was going on in a state of dreariness. But, in a moment of realisation, recalling dad's long drawn-out goodnight and goodbye before bed, I would lift the covers from my body and tiptoe out of my room to where I'd find mum on the floor.

In the corner of the hall by the front door, I remember mum's head raising one night, when her eyes caught with mine. Her arms extended to me, and she cried out even more with such sadness. I'd run and embrace her while she clenched me tight and held the back of my head with her soft motherly hand.

"My little angel," she'd say. I could feel her tears hit the crown of my head as she wept. Beside us would be our confused family pet dog and, seconds into embracing, the appearance of my younger brother. Walking up to us, he'd pat both mum and me on the head, telling us everything would be okay.

"Dad's just gone to fight the baddies, that's all. He'll be back," he said this one time.

Not acknowledging him, I cuddled into mum. I squeezed my eyes shut, trying hard to stay strong, and held her tight. I have many memories like this, but - late night and early morning comforting aside - mum was strong. Day in and day out, she made our lunches, packed our bags and dropped us at school. She picked us up, brought us home, cooked us dinner and let us stay up late. Trips to the supermarket for candy, chips and chocolate were a regular trend, with many a laugh nestled under a blanket on the couch in the living room. She always tucked us in and never forgot to tell us that she loved us. Mum could not have done better if she tried.

My brother, Luke, and I couldn't be further from comparison. He was my tough little brother, the kid in the playground who told the other boys he was a superhero while standing up to them in a costume with a mask and cape. Even when they laughed, he raised his voice as if he truly believed it and made sure they knew it. Following in our dad's footsteps, he collected army figurines, ran around the backyard shooting imaginary villains and wasn't afraid to raise his little fists to ward off bullies. I, however, collected mum's shoes, ran around the yard re-enacting scenes from fairytales as princesses in big dresses, and cowered in a corner with my eyes clenched shut if a bully confronted me, or kept my head low if I saw trouble ahead. If Luke asked me to play 'armies', I'd usually try and settle a war over a cup of tea. But no matter how different we were, our parents loved us equally, and not a day goes by I don't remember feeling that.

School was hard, both socially and educationally. Thinking back all I remember is hours and hours of holding my head and creasing my eyebrows with frustration and confusion. Lessons did seem to come as easy to me as they did with others. Mind you, when I was seated in a classroom it was better than being out at recess or lunch where I was subjected to teasing and torment. It started early too, right from grade one, as I became known as the boy who wouldn't show his penis in grade one. Innocently eating my lunch one day I was approached by a group of boys who told me they had something cool to show me. Walking with them, away from the sounds of skipping ropes on pavement, school children playing, and supervising teachers chatting, they took me to a secluded area to show me what they called 'the sex tree'.

"What's a sex tree?" I remember asking.

"Come on, I'll show you," one of them said, grabbing my hand and taking me through the bushes to the brick wall of the school building beside 'the sex tree'. The other boys followed behind us.

Even looking back now I feel cornered and claustrophobic. Up against a wall with a bunch of boys, where bushes and trees hid us. Giggling and sniggering, they all pulled their pants down. I didn't know what was going on, I was scared and uncertain. I felt helpless and didn't like not being in control. I remember starting to hyperventilate and asked to leave. Taking a few steps forward to get out, they pushed me back.

"You can't leave - you haven't showed us yours," said one of the boys.

"No," I said, turning away into the corner of the brick wall as if cuddled into mum with my eyes clenched shut.

"Michael is a scaredy cat, Michael is a scaredy cat," they taunted. They kicked dirt at me and threw twigs as they left. Although they didn't do anything further, I knew that I never wanted to feel that helpless or vulnerable ever again. I never told anyone about the event. From there on in, with every step I took around the school yard, I felt like eyes were looking at me and ready to jump. I didn't dare go to the bathroom at lunch or recess. I always made sure I held on until class time and asked the teacher for a slip out. I'd power walk to the bathroom door and look around before entering. Once inside, I'd lock the cubicle behind me. Urinals were not even an option. In a cubicle I was safe. If I ever heard the bathroom door open or footsteps walk inside, I'd tense up quickly, trying not to let anything trickle out or another breath of air escape until they left. I was left feeling anxious and cautious which, in hindsight, was not fair for a child so young to feel. It was an age I should have been fearless and ready to conquer the world. Instead, at just seven years old I started my school years hiding and cautious.

As the years rolled on I didn't make any friends. In grade two, they laughed at me because I needed special classes to help me with reading. In grade three, they laughed because I couldn't remember the order of the seasons or months, and in grade four it was because I couldn't memorise my timetables. I remember sitting at my desk in class as the teacher called each student's name to stand up and answer a sum, begging in my mind for the bell to go before it was my turn.

"Michael," the teacher called. I'd gesture a cough, or pulled a blank face.

"I'm not feeling very well this morning, miss."

"Well, get up nice and fast. The sooner you've answered your sum, the sooner you can sit back down," she said.

Up I'd get, hesitating, and looking at all the faces around the classroom with their eyes glued to me. Before the teacher even spoke my mind would fuzz. "Come on Michael, quickly," she urged.

"Sorry, miss?"

"I asked you, what is six times twelve?"

"Um-ma-ma-mm", I mumbled. I was always creasing my eyebrows and thinking out loud. Using my fingers to count, I'd forget and start again.

Hearing giggles around me, I'd forget again and have to re-count.

"Oh Michael. Sit down. If you're really sick you best not be at school, otherwise stop making excuses and start doing your homework."

The problem was, I took my homework with me every night, my mum by my side helping me as best she could. But the same problems arose; I'd lose track of my thoughts and start counting again, crease my eyebrows and think harder only to lose count. I would hear crickets in the distance, and then focus on the sounds they made as they became louder and louder in my head.

"Okay Michael. Let's call it a night shall we?" mum often said.

I did end up getting tutoring but by then it was too late as the teachers assumed I didn't pay attention and the students thought I was a laughing stock. I settled in to the discomfort. I gave up on myself.

Above all, sports was the worst, I hated sports with a passion. It may have been related to my experience in grade one, but I never wanted to shower. I did everything I could to avoid being vulnerable. I avoided being bare naked. Made to feel uncomfortable about my body. I wore my sports shirt underneath my uniform, but then I got told off. I went a demountable classroom, to take my school shirt off and put my sports shirt on, but then I got caught out.

"Michael, when you play sports, you sweat, and when you sweat you soap up," my sports teacher said. Event after event, my whole primary school life was tense and unfair. While others ran amuck, made friends and arranged play dates on the weekend, I sat alone, read books, and most weekends were spent with the family – not that I disliked that as I considered my mum my best friend. There were, however, countless times that I came home or got in the car and burst into tears. Mum was so comforting and always knew how to cheer me up, but it didn't change the hours each day I had to tolerate the nastiness of the kids at school. Climbing the grades of primary school, I started to adopt an attitude. It did get me into strife with the principal and my teachers, but what would you expect when you're a child who's been tormented for years and years on end? The worst part was that it went on unnoticed.

In grade five, in the playground, I was sitting on a bench in the undercover area as a student in a wheelchair approached me.

"What are you doing?" He asked.

"Reading," I answered begrudgingly, as he'd teased me before. Sure, he was in a wheelchair, but he fit in with the others and felt the need to join in on their cruelties.

"What, you don't want to play, little dumb dumb?"

"I'm not a dumb dumb!"

"Why you reading then, catching up on your times tables are we?" He rolled the wheels of his chair closer and snatched the book off me.

"Can you please give that back?"

"It's not even a school book - it's about aaaa," he paused squinting his eyes to read a line. "Plug it up? A girls period. What a freak you are. What are you doing reading about periods! Hey, guys..." He called out to the other boys in the playground.

"Hey!" I interrupted, snatching the book back off him. He turned back around to face me, and wheeled his way forward. I'd jumped up onto the bench and started to laugh. Right there and then, up on that bench, I was in control.

"What are you going to do now - come up here and snatch it?!" I was the one sniggering for once. For the first time. "You can't, can you?!" I shouted. I laughed some more, as a teacher approached.

"Michael!" the teacher shouted in an authoritative manner. The boy looked away from me and down to his lap as if upset. "What do you think you're doing?"

"I didn't start..."

"I don't care who started it, Michael. What you have done is extremely ill-mannered and not tolerated at all. I will be sending you to the principal and your mother can come and collect you from his office after school."

The boy in the wheelchair looked up at me and grinned. How could a boy so cruel and provoking get away with something like that? I took it too far, yes, but I was a kid and I reacted in defense.

*

That afternoon, I spent the rest of my time at school at a small desk in the principal's office writing the sentence, *it is wrong to tease others about their disabilities*, over and over again until my mum came to get me. When mum got there she looked shocked. She walked into the room and our eyes caught for a moment while I gave her a look to let her know I was sorry. Her facial expression didn't provide much for comfort. She sat down on a chair in front of the principal's desk and then he addressed me.

"Well, Michael, put the pencil down and come join us," he said. I walked over as if ashamed. But why was I? I was the one who had been targeted, and all I did was react. It was one of those moments where the senior person laid down the law and I was refused any argument on the matter, with no chance to justify my actions, having to accept what I did was wrong. My mum spent the meeting shaking her head and looking at me in disbelief and disappointment. The drive home was completely silent. Dinner that night was unsettling, and when I went to speak mum asked me not to.

"What did Mikey do, mummy?" Luke asked, seated at the dinner table with us.

"Something he ought not to have done. He teased a defenceless boy, rather than sticking up for him like you would have Luke," she said.

"He..." I went to speak.

"Not a word, Michael," she interrupted.

"This isn't fair," I said.

"Right, off to your room. You obviously didn't hear a thing your principal said and you obviously don't have any remorse about what you did."

I looked at mum for a moment, and then stormed off to my room. I leapt onto my bed, with my head buried into the pillow as tears streamed from my eyes. Mum came into my room later that night and, although she said she loved me, she also said she expected me to apologise to the boy and mean it. So, I did, but I didn't mean it for a second.

*

In grade six, I was out on the field playing baseball. Another day in hell. At this stage, all I wanted was to get through school, get through life, and die. I truly did.

"All right Michael, you're up," the sports teacher yelled. Standing off to the side, I walked up to the rack of baseball clubs, grabbed one and walked into position. Ahead of me was some smart arse kid, someone who always had a good laugh at my expense. I lined my sight up, let go of the club to adjust my cap and heard a *WOOSH* as the ball went straight past me.

"Sir, I wasn't ready," I shouted.

"Well, Michael, get ready. Go fetch the ball, will you?" I looked around at my sniggering peers.

"Yeah, go fetch it," murmured the smart arse under his breath. Unable to retaliate, I turned my back and went to get the ball. The game continued, and every step I took was agony. The sun was scorching, anxiety and frustration started to kick in, and a feeling of hopelessness – which was almost always present that year – festered within me even more so in that moment, slouching with every step I took. The game felt like it went on forever, and then the time came for me to take the ball. *Great. I'm not going to*

throw it right, I'm going to use the wrong technique, or my aim is going to be way off. I
approached centre field with the ball gripped in my hand and looked down
at its stitching for a few seconds. So imperfect, some stitches wider than
others and some stitches loose while others remained tight. Remember
thinking they kind of resembled how I felt. Jiggered and all over the place.

"Michael, we're waiting," the sports teacher said, unenthusiastically.

As I looked up and ahead, there he was right in front of me, the
smart arse, with his perfect blonde shining hair shimmering in the sunlight.
I wondered if this day could have gotten any worse. But then, I had a
moment of spontaneous thought, as if someone had flicked a switch in my
head. *Lob it at him, right in his noggin,* I thought. You're in control now. If I
get him right between the eyes, it will be a nice treat for his folks. I
imagined the stream of blood that would have gushed down his face as the
weight of the baseball slammed up against his face. Lining up the pitch, I
brought the ball up to my eye line. I unhunched my slouched posture, took
a short jog back, turned around and then ran with might! As quick as I
started to run the ball left my hand, and as quick as it left my hand it passed
the smart arse right by his head as it had mine moments before. *Nooooo!
Damn it!* For a moment, the smart arse's eyes widened as if he knew what I
had meant to do, then his expression turned into a grin and chuckle as he
looked around at our peers and then back at me.

"What the hell was that?!" What the hell indeed.

*

Grade seven sucked as much as the whole of primary school combined. How I couldn't wait to get away from these supposed classmates of mine. If there was anything that came out good for me this year it was my newfound love for music. I'd always dabbled in drama and arts, taking part in the school play if one was produced and enrolling in holiday drama courses. This year, after much debate with the school psychologist to start some kind of recreational activity, I joined the school choir. I didn't mind it to be fair. There were a few folks I stayed clear from, but there were people in other years which I conversed with from time to time. Singing seemed to ease my stress, calm my state and take my mind off of the hell hole I felt I was living. Music had been the key the whole time, but it was only then that I discovered it. After just two months, I proposed a talent quest to my choir instructor, of whom I had formed a great relationship with in the time I'd been attending. She took my idea on with great interest and set a date and time for auditions. She booked out the school hall for me and have me the responsibility to promote and market it to the students.

I was so excited. I had found a passion and love for something other than my family, and a space where I felt somewhat accepted. Embraced by musical notes. I was finally going home to practice and work, instead of crying in self pity. I took some time out in the library to read up on coordinating events, looked up the process of auditions, and then hopped onto the computer to create a notice. I slipped the notices under the doors of the classrooms and posted them on windows around the schoolyard. The notice detailed the time and place to meet, and before I knew it the day had arrived. I woke up determined, remembering precisely what my choir instructor had told me to do.

"Remember, Michael, just before lunch I will unlock the hall for you. As a senior I am trusting you to supervise anyone that shows up to audition and ask them to register on the registration form. Then, take a seat until I return." That whole morning I sat with my eyes stuck to the clock, flicking my pencil back and forth waiting for the lunch time bell. When the bell rang, I sprinted to the hall as fast I could, opened the door and sat down at a desk to take registrations. Two students came in, the first for singing and the second for playing clarinet. Then shortly after, the smart arse and his pals turned up. They waltzed in as if it were their own home, and the smart arse placed his hands across from me on the desk I was sat.

"Well-ah, it looks like you've got a pretty popular talent quest going on here, Michael," he said sarcastically.

"More people are on their way," I said.

"Oh, really?" the smart arse responded as he stepped back with his pals, "there might not be enough room once we get the spots – hey, boys?"

"You're not here to audition."

"Oh, yeah? Who says?" He asked, not caring for an answer. He and the others started to run around singing stupid songs like idiots. In the corner of my eye I saw a girl come to the door who then shied away upon seeing the boys running around. All of a sudden the feelings of anxiety, frustration and hopelessness returned to my body. I was disturbed and upset. My enthusiasm ripped itself apart. I felt heat build within me, small pin like pricks covered my body and my muscles began to tense all over. The boys continued to run around. I stood up from my seat and walked around to the front of the table pointing at the door with my pencil as if a teacher.

"GET OUT!" I screamed. The boys stopped what they were doing, and approached me slowly.

"What did you say?" asked the smart arse, his face coming into close proximity with mine. My fist tightened around the pencil, and my arm moved in one swift action jabbing the pencil into his shoulder.

"Get out! Get out! Get out!" I shouted as I continued to jab the pencil back and forth, jabbing and missing, jabbing and missing. He shielded himself with his arms as all the students in the room, including his boys, stood back and watched.

"Michael!" The choir instructor screamed as she walked into the hall. The smart arse held his shoulder, holding back actual tears. The instructor ran up to him and started to escort him out, before turning back to face me. "Do not move - I will be back for you! As for the Talent Quest, better luck with it in high school. Come on, boys – the principal is going to need some statements."

It really sucked. I had felt an uncontrollable urge come over me and just lost it. Again, I was provoked. All I kept thinking was the grief he and his friends had caused me over the years. They had been the ones behind the bushes in grade one – by 'the sex tree'. Grown side by side as bullies. The one thing I had finally found enjoyment in at school, the one thing I was proudly involved with which was something I had put all my energy and passion into, and they just had to come in and ruin it for me.

*

The rest of the year saw me attending regular psychology sessions, and dealing with a worried mum who was concerned for me almost consistently. My psychologist taught me coping strategies for anxiety and ways to challenge my thoughts. Which sounded great in theory, but didn't work so well when put into practice for a teased and taunted schoolboy. Home time became unproductive, yet again, but I had no more tears to dispense. Rides home in the car with mum went from tears, to frozen emotionless and un-invested conversation. One night, I woke in my bed to cries yet again. Much older now, I did not raise my blankets, but sat myself up. Listening carefully, I heard both mum and dad's voices from the kitchen. I quietly walked my way down the hallway where I stood and listened beside the doorframe. Mum was a mess, crying to dad asking why *I* wasn't happy.

"Why is Michael like this? Why can't he just be a happy kid? It's not right - it's not how children should feel." I stood there with tears starting to form once again, not for myself but at the thought of how I had made my mum feel. I tiptoed back to my room, pulled the covers over my head, and pushed my face into my pillow. I remember sobbing many tears that night. The thought of hurting someone I loved – my mum of all people – hurt so much more than I had been hurt by any bully.

That next morning I woke with an ambition to please her. I got up out of bed and walked into the kitchen. As I made myself breakfast, mum approached and wrapped her arms around me from behind.

"Good morning, my little angel. How are you this morning?"

"Morning, mum. I'm feeling really good today," I said with a smile. Mum manoeuvred my body around, turning me to face her and grabbed my shoulders either side.

"Yeah?"

"Yeah," I smiled again. "I feel like life can only get better from here. I've only got a few months left of primary school, and then it's a fresh start."

Mum smiled and pulled me close as she stroked my head. Of course I didn't mean it, but I was protecting her from my feelings. After all, mum really was the most important person in my life, and the thought of hurting her was unbearable. I didn't see leaving primary school and venturing off to high school as a fresh start at all. I found it terrifying.

*

The final month of school approached, and all anyone was talking about was the school dance, the event that finished it all. Except me, of course, as I sat reading my books alone at lunch. I must admit it was the books that got me through primary school. Each and every book I read gave me the opportunity to escape reality, to hop out of this world into another, where I didn't have to be *me* for a brief few crispy pages.

The couple of weeks that proceeded were okay. I wasn't bothered too much after attacking the smart arse with a pencil - in fact, quite the opposite, my peers mostly left me alone. I'd walk down a corridor and they almost seemed to avoid eye contact with me and even moved to get further away. While I sensed a little fear, I mostly think it was just a different tactic to try to make me feel like an outsider as they stepped *obviously* away.

Before I knew it, it was the final week of school – ever! Then, the night of the school dance arrived, and that afternoon our classroom teacher reminded us all to dress nicely for the evening.

"No shorts and no jeans. This is a dance, not a barbecue," said the teacher. I sat at my desk for a moment longer after the bell rang while the students around me got up to leave. Although I hadn't made any friends and although I had not shared good times with my peers, I felt a small sentimental moment of realisation that primary school was almost over. Whether it was because I was leaving all these nasty peers behind me, or whether it was because I was taking the next step in my life, I do not know. But that feeling, of what I look back on now and would almost describe as an accomplishment, felt good. I remember smiling to myself as I sat at that desk while the rest of the students ran out from that classroom. Perhaps, it was wasn't accomplishment I felt, but survival.

On my way home, mum took me to a hair appointment she had

booked for me. Sitting in the chair at the salon I expected my normal trim.

"Whatever you want - this is your big night," mum said, to my surprise. "If you want it coloured, tinted, or cut in a different style, go for it! No matter the cost!"

"Really?"

"Yes, Michael, have fun with it," she replied. I wasn't quite sure, nor was I ready to get something completely different to my normal trim. However, I did think of something, and I smiled again for the second time that day.

*

In the car, back out in front of the school, I dreaded to go to that dance.

"Michael, it looks great, people won't even notice it with all the coloured flashing disco lights," said mum, trying to boost my confidence. I pulled down the car visor and looked into the mirror. It hadn't turned out like I'd wanted, but I suppose it wasn't too bad. It was also one of the last nights I had to spend with these peers of mine, and why should I have let them get in the way of me having a good night? Music had become a love of mine, and that's what tonight was going to be full of. Music and dancing. With that in mind, I looked at mum with a smile.

"Thanks mum," I said, mostly to please her.

"I will be back out here at ten o'clock, all right?" checked mum.

"Right," I responded. I got out of the car, waving back at her as she drove off, when a sudden deep feeling of distress weighed itself deep down into the bottom of my gut. I started to walk towards the hall, and I could already hear the sniggering of peers as they got out from their parents cars and walked by me. In pairs and clusters, having come with their friends, they pointed at me as they walked ahead. I took a deep breath through my nose as advised by the psychologist. I held the breath for three seconds, and exhaled out through my mouth. Walking on, I continued to do this a few more times. As I reached the hall, there was the smart arse and his date leaning up against the wall near the entrance. The smart arse looked at me. He burst into laughter, wrapped his hands around his mouth and ran inside dragging his date by her hand behind him. She too took a glance at me and had laughed. I stood, took one more inhale, held it for three more seconds, resisting my feelings of anxiety, then exhaled before I marched on inside.

Walking into the dance was the most humiliating and horrible feeling I had ever experienced at that point in my life. As I stepped inside, the smart arse's date switched the hall lights on. The hall filled with light as bright as day. In front of me, my peers gathered around. They all blew party poppers at me and started chanting 'raaaaanga, raaaaanga, raaaaanga'. Being

a dark-haired boy, I looked at guys with blonde hair all my childhood with

envy. I don't know why. I just had. When I'd gone to the hairdresser and

mum said I could have anything I wanted, I asked the hairdresser to dye my

hair blonde. Naturally dark, it turned auburn, like an orange rust. Mum, in

her kindness, and not wanting to break my spirit must have nodded at the

hairdresser as I do recall them having started to speak. I looked around as

they all chanted the word *ranga* over and over as they pointed and laughed.

The smart arse was front and centre, and walked up to shake my hand.

"Congratulations, Michael. You successfully turned yourself into an

ape – a real way to finish school. Hey! Don't stab me now," he said, as he

stepped backwards, hesitating to get closer, but still determined to push my

limits. If I wasn't already, I had truly become the school joke.

"What is the meaning of this?" Asked a teacher on duty, as they

walked inside. The other teachers followed behind, looking around starting

to quiet the students down around me.

I lost it. I mean, really lost it. I felt anxiety and distress building

within me, my calves tensed, my shoulders tightened and my mind felt as if

it was going to explode. I ran over to a buffet that was laid out and started

throwing trays of food around, grabbing dishes with canapés and throwing

them into the air. I grabbed the punch bowl of fruit juice, turning to try and throw it at them all, but as I rose it above my head I'd became unbalanced, and instead poured it over myself. The fruit juice hit the floor and then the punch bowl followed as it smashed into pieces across the ground. Covered in food and punch, my hair and clothes were drenched. I yelled out loudly, and the teachers didn't stop me, in fact they stood and watched with my now ex-peers. The hall turned from laughter and chanting, to silence.

"Why don't you like me?! Why don't any of you like me?!" I screamed as they all stared with blank looks on their faces. "What did I ever do wrong? How did I ever make any one of you feel like I had to be treated like this?! All I ever wanted was a friend." I started to lower my voice and walk up to the cluster of them. "I just wanted to be blonde tonight. I thought some of you might have liked me better or come up and, god forbid, talked to me, but even a gesture isn't good enough for any of you!"

"Wasn't a very good gesture, was it?" The smart arse sniggered.

"Out!" Shouted one of the teachers. Smart arse jumped at the teachers order and left the hall quickly. I looked around the hall. Why was I even bothering to get through to them? None of them were worth anything to me.

"Michael, let's call your mum," said one of the teachers as they cautiously approached me and put their arms out to comfort me.

"Don't come near me," I said. "In seven years you never once helped. You're as bad as this lot." I walked out of the hall and passed smart arse leaning up against the wall. I caught his eye and I leapt towards him. He flinched. I laughed before continuing to sob, and then walked onward, away from the hall. Away from what had been my hell hole, for the very last time. On my journey home, I stopped by a park and laid down on the grass for a few minutes, looking up at the night sky. The stars were glistening, they attracted me so. I started to take a few more deep breaths, and then stopped. What a bunch of crap, I thought to myself. I sat up and looked over at the street ahead, there were a couple of older teenagers illuminated by the yellow glow of street lights while walking along chatting amongst each other. Their arms were linked, and they giggled at each others words. *That's all I want. Just a friend*, I remember thinking.

*

I got home shortly before nine o'clock and knocked on the door. Dad opened it.

"Mate," he said, looking up and down at the state of me. Now with grass stuck to my clothes. "What happened to you?"

"I don't want to talk about it."

"Honey, who's that?" Mum called out.

41

"It's Michael, he's back early," dad called back. I ran off to the bathroom before mum had a chance to see me and locked the door. I undressed and dumped my clothes in the bathtub, leaning on the bench of the basin while I looked at myself in the mirror. I was shaking, and breathed deeply, trying to stop myself from crying. I walked over to the shower and turned it on. Then, there was a knock on the door.

"Is everything all right angel?" Mum asked.

"Yes, mum, everything's fine. It just wasn't for me, that's all," I said, trying the control myself and my breath, trying to not upset her. Before I got into the shower, I walked back to the bench and bent down to open up the basin doors. I reached behind the shampoo bottles and spare packets of toothpaste to the back of the cupboard where I had stored a kitchen knife. I'd wrapped it up in a hand towel. I pulled it out and slowly unwrapped it, grabbing the knife by its handle, and letting the hand towel drop to the floor. I looked at the blade of the knife, turned and twisted it as the light caught it at various angles, then firmly held it upright. I stood in front of the mirror and stared at myself while the bathroom started to fill with steam. For a while, I just blankly looked ahead. I stood in contemplation and wonder as a young man with nothing but possibilities ahead of him. I got the knife, taking the tip of its point to the edge of my wrist. I didn't apply pressure, but ran it slowly up my arm and then back down to my wrist, then lightly circled its point over it. It calmed me. It felt like a light tickle. I shut my eyes, and for a split second I considered pushing the knife into my flesh and dragging the knife down my arm. Then, I imagined the occurrences which would take place after that. My mind leapt ahead, and it stopped me from continuing to do anything drastic. I pictured my mum walking in on my body on the cold tiled bathroom floor covered in blood. At the thought of her, I began to shed a tear. I dropped the knife, leant forward and held myself up on the bench. Sniffing and breathing heavily I wiped my nose and took another deep inhale. There was a knock at the door again.

"Michael! Are you okay? I heard a clang," mum called out.

"Yes, mum, I just went to turn the water off and the shower handle fell off" I responded, thinking quickly on my feet.

"Well, all right." She paused for a moment. "I love you… Michael."

I pictured my mum's beautiful face. Although on the other side of the door, it was as if she was standing right in front of me. With such love and devotion for me, her little angel as she'd say.

"I love you too, mum."

Sitting here, now, at my dresser with the conceptualisation of what I wanted to do to those queens. I did wonder just how far the unconditional love of a mother really stretched, and what her thoughts would have been were I to go through with it. Certainly, *not,* her little angel.

3 A PLACE OF REFUGE

Believe it or not, high school was the start of a brand new era for me. Accepted as a late applicant into a school of the arts, with a hard push from my mother, I entered a place of refuge. Accepted into a program for Musical Theatre, I was told that I had a natural flair for performance. I felt rather chuffed.

I remember the audition day as clearly as a summer day. Mum drove me, and the whole way there I was filled with excitement and happiness. I was so thrilled not having to continue schooling with my primary peers. If I could get into this specialist high school, a true fresh start awaited me. Mum had been so encouraging, listening to me sing and telling me how talented I was. As we drove up to the entrance I beamed with positivity. Mum placed her hand on my knee and looked over at me.

"This is it, baby - your chance to shine," she said. We pulled into a car bay at the front of the school. Mum undid her belt, swivelled herself around on the driver's seat and grabbed both of my hands firmly. "No matter what goes on in there, Michael, just know that there's always a window that opens once a door closes behind you, and if things don't go so well, then it is just not your time. Fate will have something else miraculous out there ready and waiting for you, okay?"

"Thanks, mum," I smiled. But this time my smile was genuine, to the point that I felt if I smiled any more my cheeks would have split.

"But I know you're going to do great, and you just need to go in there and show them the beautiful boy I know so well," she added. Mum leant over to hug me and I embraced her. Her hugs were always the most comforting, and I got so much strength from them.

Getting out of the car I looked back, waving. Mum waved back so proud, yet I could sense her nerves as she brought her hands back to her chest, clenching them in hope. As I walked on, ahead of me was a building which looked a billion times bigger than my primary school. It was multi-storey and stood high above the trees. In front of it was a stairway which I started to walk up. Looking to the top of the building, my foot stumped a step and I tripped. A student not too far behind me quickly sped up to assist me.

"Are you okay?" they asked.

"Yeah, thanks. I'm fine," I said. The student smiled and walked ahead. I was in shock that I had tripped and was actually helped as opposed to made fun of. I continued up the steps with confidence, and once I reached the top walked towards a pair of large double doors. A sign beside them read, *Semester One Auditions – Room 106, Second Floor.* I walked through the doors and inside was filled with students both tall and short. Groups of friends sat with musical instruments, and multiple people sat reading books. The energy inside this place was pulsing with creativeness and mateship. I took a deep inhale, but not for my anxiety. It was a breath to take in that moment.

Finding the room was difficult. I got lost multiple times, and asked for directions from both teachers and students. Finally making it, I approached the door. The numbers 106 stuck out to me as if they were a vital piece to a puzzle that was the rest of my life. Beside the door were a couple of other auditionees. As I got to the door they made eye contact and openly greeted me.

"Hi, I'm Simon," one of the guys said, introducing himself with his hand held out. I shook it, and introduced myself. The others introduced themselves too, some with a handshake and some with a gesture of a salute like wave. These guys were friendly and, most of all, they were engaging with me. Kindly. No muscle in my body felt tense, and I genuinely felt normal. As I listened to each of these guys talk to one another, I looked at their expressions. It was the first moment in my life I had felt accepted. They weren't 'friends', but they were enough. The door to room 106 opened, and from it walked a man with a moustache, checkered shirt and jeans.

"All right boys, come on in," he said.

I walked in with the seven other guys, into a room which looked nothing special. It was dated, with old green carpet and cream painted walls that were chipped. The window frames had also been painted over, and had flakes missing on parts which exposed old blue metal. But what the room had was a sense of comfort, and it felt like this was where I was meant to be.

"Okay guys, take a seat," the man said. As we each took a spot on the floor with no seats in sight, I looked in front of us where two trestle tables had been positioned with three adults seated behind them. The man that invited us in was sitting on the edge of the table to our left. In total there were four teachers seated in front of us, ready to determine our futures. *Please oh please oh please*, I thought, let this be the place I spend the next part of my life. My nerves were uncontrollable, but I let them take me on the ride, as they weren't nerves of distress, but hope.

"So," said the man, "this is where some of you will be spending the next five years of your lives. Welcome to *Lumiere College of the Arts!* Here, if successful on entry, you will gain the skills, knowledge, abilities and power to pursue a career in the spotlight upon graduation. However, this does not come without responsibilities. As a student at Lumiere, you are expected to keep up your grades, keep on top of your homework and keep up your attendance."

The words 'grades' and 'homework' hit a cord with me. I gulped. But something inside me said I could do this. This is your time, you will rise to it, it said.

"Today, each of us will take you as a group through four aspects of musical theatre," he continued. "You will keep up, listen and take direction when directed. After the four sessions you will be given the chance to break where we have some sandwiches and drinks ordered for you. You will then be given a tour of the facilities, returning here for your official audition examination."

The next few hours saw us following directions from each individual on the panel. As each adult took us for their own time, while the others assessed and wrote notes. Looking at each of us from one to the other, their eyes continued to shift, their pens kept noting and their pages kept turning. The man who welcomed us was Mr Culver. He had a classic moustache, and clothes which seemed as if they had been in his wardrobe since he graduated high school himself. Mr Culver directed us through the precision of characterisation, otherwise known as how to hold oneself and how to project a character onto your audience. He led with large movements and over-exaggerated expressions.

Next up was a session in pronunciation, directed by Miss Fitz; a lady with frizzy, short hair and half-circle spectacles on the tip of her nose. She handed us each a sheet of paper with phrases and vowels. Standing at the front of the room, she held her own sheet in front of her, looking down at the page as she read and then back up to us to demonstrate. She continued to pronounce and project the phrases on the page as we followed. Her lips were like elastic; they stretched wide and far and were as thin and narrow as a duck's beak. Each of us stood in a line, glanced at each other with a slight smirk, giggling under our breath, but quickly looked back to the front as Mr Culver cleared his throat.

Session three took us into song. As Miss Fitz took her seat, the woman sat beside her placed her palms on the table and pushed herself up leaning forward as she looked at each of us. As she spoke her head was turned down but her eyes looked up and forward. She had a petite blonde bob which fell forward as she leant.

"Throughout history, it has been the inaction of those who could have acted, the indifference of those who should have known better, and the silence of the voice of justice when it mattered most, that has made it possible for evil to triumph. The Emperor of Ethiopia, Haile Selassie, said this. I say let it out," she said. She raised her head and stood up, walking around the table to the front of it. She leaned back, sitting on its edge and folded her arms. She was younger and trendy adult, possibly an ex-goth. She wore a dark shade of lipstick, a black blouse and skin tight jeans the shade of ash, with black knee high boots that had small heels.

"Speak up! Be not afraid and let it out in song! Mrs Cornell is my name and, if granted a place with us, I will take you through to carry your voice to the other ends of the earth. Open up and project, release and embrace. The voice is your soul, and your connection with it."

She clapped her hands in one loud and powerful clap. "Close it up, and it'll be lost forever. Open it up, and let the good times roll," she said as she stood from the desk and raised her fist in the air. She laughed and started to pace back and forth. She went on to explain that the voice was an instrument, and that you had to use it to benefit from it. The session entailed vocal warm-ups, exercises and singing along with some light choreography. It was intense, but then so was she. She got out of me tunes I never even realised I was capable of projecting. Maybe I was wrapped up in my own head, but I felt like she warmed to me. Looked at me more frequently than the others. Even engaged me with a wink at one point.

The final session was with another man, Mr Stanley. This man was squeamish and quiet, yet showed signs of confidence. British and book-wormish, he wore an old brown librarian-like suit, vest and tie. He wore rounded glasses and had a full-grown beard. Standing from his seat, he cleared his throat with his fist held underneath his nose and walked in front of us. He explained the importance of the history of the theatre, music and the arts. If selected, he would be our arts historian.

After our last session we broke for our feed, and the guys and I talked about the characteristics of the teachers, what we enjoyed and what we hadn't. It was really nice to have guys my age to share my experiences with. Afterwards, we were collected by the Dean of the Arts, Ms Martinovich. Ms Martinovich seemed almost as if she could have been Mr Stanley's wife, as she too wore what I'd describe as a librarian-like suit, though slightly more modern and a light shade of grey. She held herself strong and was extremely well spoken. Her hair was sheet-white, and her skin wrinkly yet firm. Walking us round the school she showed confidence, and finished the tour in the school's main auditorium. As I stood in the theatre, I looked around at the hundreds of seats, the stage, the curtains and a rig of canned lights. This space was my future, the stage was where I wanted to be. As Ms Martinovich spoke about the history of the school, the boys looked around, and I wandered up onto the stage where I looked out to the seating. A spotlight switched on, almost blinding me as it pointed directly towards me. I lifted my hands to block the initial shine, and then lowered them as I stared ahead. Time froze for a moment with a flicker of coloured lights, as the room filled with an applauding audience. I imagined myself briefly as the star of a production. All eyes on me, in delight and gratitude. Then back to reality.

"Michael?" Ms Martinovich asked.

"Yeah?" I responded.

"I asked, how does it feel?"

"Sorry?"

"How does it feel? To have the spotlight shine on your skin?" She asked from the back of the theatre, pointing the spotlight at me. I smiled.

"Great, Miss," I said. "It feels great."

*

Back in room 106, they each thanked us for our time, and let us know that if we were not offered a place at the school that this was not the end of our journey. I sat with my ears and eyes wide open, taking in every last second I could while I was there. Each of us were then asked to take a seat outside, where we would be called back in one by one. We left as a group. I could sense the hope in each of the guys I had just spent the day with. I looked at them and spoke.

"Good luck, guys. You're all going to do great." They smiled and looked back down to the floor, or paced with their eyes shut, humming notes and practicing their projection. I just sat there looking at what was happening around me, not sure what to do. The guy who first introduced himself to me, Simon, was called in first. The waiting became a little nerve-wrecking. Time passed, and my mind fuzzed. Then all of a sudden, my name was called.

"Michael," called Mr Culver. I looked up at him and stood, taking my last deep breath for that day. I walked into the room where the three teachers were sat once again. Mr Culver passed me on his way back to the table and asked me to stand in the centre of the room. I took my place and stood with my shoulders back and head held high.

"Michael," Mr Culver addressed me, sitting down as he tucked his chair in.

"Yes, sir?" I replied.

"We've been watching you today, Michael. You have a natural flair for performance," he said.

I smiled. "Thank you, sir."

"But we've been looking at your grades from your previous school and we're a little concerned." I started to fret. For the first time that day, my stomach turned. "I suppose what I'm trying to say here is that if we are to proceed with this audition, and you were accepted, you'd need to really pull your weight".

"Oh yes, sir. I can, I will!" I responded. Mr Culver looked over to the panel by his side. They looked at him and then back to me. Mr Stanley then proceeded to speak.

"Michael, I know you. You're that passionate kid who would promise anyone the world to do what he wants. But when we say you need to pull you weight, you really need to commit to this. Can you do that?" He asked.

"I believe I can, sir," I said with complete want and need for it.

"All right, then. Let's proceed," concluded Mr. Stanley.

The next part was a blur. I sung, I recited and I moved. But as for the details, I honestly cannot recall them. What I do recall is finishing, and standing in silence with my mind running one hundred miles an hour. I stood and looked at the teachers while they finished their notes on their papers occasionally glancing up at me and each other. The silence was deafening.

"Sorry, if I could, I'd just like to say something," I said. The teachers looked up. Mr Culver sat back and folded his arms, Ms Fitz leaned forward and took her glasses off of her nose, Mrs Cornel placed her right arm on the table and leaned her chin on her knuckles with her fingers wound to a fist, and Mr Stanley rested his right hand on top of his left while tilting his head to the side in interest.

"Throughout my whole life, I have never felt accepted. Today when I walked into these doors, I felt like I found a place of acceptance. All through primary school I was teased and tormented for being different. For not kicking a ball with the others at lunch. Here I already feel this enormous support, and I've been here not even a day. I need this. I'm so close to..." I paused. "I need a place like this."

"And you're certain you can pick up your grades, Michael?" Ms Fitz asked.

"Ms Fitz, I'm not certain of anything, but I'm going to try. I will try and try as best I can. If that means skipping outings to the movies to stay home and read then so be it. I want in," I pleaded. Mrs Cornel stood up from her seat, walked around the table towards me and put her hand out in front of me.

"Then welcome to Lumiere," she said. I looked at her hand and then up at her. She grinned. Holding my tears back, I bypassed her hand and hugged her. She hesitated for a moment, but then placed her arms around me. As much as I tried to fight back those tears, they just started to roll out. But they were tears of relief and happiness. Finally, something good had happened in my life.

4 FIRST KISS

I will never forget the thrill and excitement my mum shared with me when I told her I was accepted to Lumiere.

"When your dad gets back tomorrow we're going to go out to dinner and celebrate," she said. I was glowing. I had turned a new leaf and I was not going to let anyone get me down. This school was the start of something bigger and better for me, I just knew it. We were booked into a restaurant we went to regularly. My dad called it Clifford's Palace, as that was his name. Dad was a real character, always a great host and usually the springer of conversation. The restaurant was nice, it was familiar to me, and the walls were draped in pretty coloured fabrics which I loved. Sat at the table I looked over at dad as he ordered the family our meals. Always friendly and joking with the waiter, dad had a rather infectious chuckle. I looked over at mum to my left, and my brother to my right. We were a tight family, and I was so happy to be part of it.

"Hear hear, guys," said dad, raising his glass. We each grabbed our drinks and held them as dad spoke. "We're awfully proud of you, Michael. To have gotten into this school is really something, and I hope you know that. Congratulations, matey." I felt very special, and raised my glass with them as we cheered and each took a sip. Mum reached over and placed her hand on mine.

"We really are so proud of you," she said.

"I'm proud of you too, Mikey," said Luke, smiling so wide that you could see all of his teeth. I thanked him, and we all indulged in a great meal while sharing in a good time.

For the rest of the break leading up to the start of semester, I spent my days practicing my vocals and going over what I learnt in the one day I spent at Lumiere. Mum rented CDs from the library for me, and I spent many afternoons laying on my bed with an old Discman, listening to scores upon scores from many a musical. My three favourites were Andrew Lloyd Weber's Phantom of the Opera, Jesus Christ Superstar and Cats. Listening to these tracks made my body feel things it had never felt before and the music sent tingles up my spine. As I closed my eyes I clenched them, not in stress but in feeling the notes which the tracks released.

*

On the morning of semester one, I virtually hopped out of bed and made my way to the kitchen where dad had made me bacon and eggs. Mum was standing in the kitchen by his side with a cup of coffee in her hands. They both looked at me, smiling.

"Ready for your big day?" Mum asked.

"Am I ever!" I responded. I raced over to mum and gave her a big hug. "Good morning, mum! Good morning, dad!" Dad chuckled.

"Good morning, my little angel," mum said as she placed her coffee down on the bench and embraced in my hug.

"I don't know if he's so little anymore, mumma, he'll be taller than you pretty soon I'd say," said dad. Mum slapped dad softly on the arm.

"He'll always be my little angel. Won't you, sweetie?" she asked as she grabbed my chin.

"Always," I said. I walked over to the table and poured myself a big glass of juice. Dad walked over with the pan and served me breakfast with a pair of tongs, dropping a piece of bacon as Luke came running into the room and wrestled dad from behind.

"Careful mister," Mum said.

"Sorry, mum," Luke said. Dad put the pan down and started to wrestle Luke down to the floor.

"It's okay. He didn't mean anything by it," dad said. Mum laughed and sat down at the table with me. I looked over at dad as he wrestled with my little brother. They were so close, just like mum and I. I was glad both mum and dad had a child they each bonded with, but most of all I was just glad we all got on. Now that I didn't have primary school to worry about, I was really looking forward to enjoying these moments more, not having to think about my peers or the stress of going to school each day.

"Now Michael, remember what we discussed?" asked mum. "Today I will drop you at the bus stop. Once you get on, take it all the way to the main station where your next bus will pick you up from platform five and then take you directly to school, okay?"

"Yep, I've got it," I said. Being a specialist school, it wasn't as close as if I had have gone to the local high school. But I didn't care, it felt worth the commute.

When Mum dropped me at the bus stop that day, the walk from the car to the bus stop was a moment of transition for me. I walked, looking back to wave at mum. She waved back fast with a drastic smile on her face. When I reached the bus stop I waited for a while, looking down at my feet, down the road, and then back at my feet. As the bus started approaching, I put my hand out to hail it. The doors to the bus opened and inside was an older-looking man, bald on top with stubble around his face.

"Where to, kid?" the bus driver asked.

"The main station, thanks," I said, as I walked on happily. He asked for three dollars and eighty cents, I gave him a twenty dollar note as that's what mum had given me. He looked at it begrudgingly.

"You got anything else?" He asked.

"No sir, just this," I said.

"All right, just get on, but next time I want change, kid," he said demandingly. I nodded and walked on, putting the money back in my pocket. The bus wasn't too full, which gave me a full range of seats to choose from.

I sat by a window and looked outside as the bus drove off. I had brought a book with me for the ride, but I was quite content to just look out onto the passing world. Once I arrived at the station, I got off and thanked the bus driver. He gave me a glare through his rear vision mirror, but didn't say anything back. I walked off and on to find platform five. On my way I saw other students in Lumiere uniforms. I followed them, not too closely, but close enough to keep up and, as you'd have guessed it, they led me straight there. As I waited for the next bus, more and more students gathered at the platform. Some knew each other and chatted, while some stood alone like me. I wasn't very fazed, and I was honestly quite content observing. Then, as the bus pulled in, the students scampered, pushed and pulled. The doors opened up, and there was a mad rush to get on. I didn't see why, so I just continued to patiently wait. As the line died down, I got on board, where I was greeted by a lady much nicer than the gentleman before.

"Well, go on then, get up there," she said.

"But there's nowhere to sit," I said.

"Hence the mad rush to get on. But you're a young lad - your legs can handle it. Go on then, up the aisle." I looked side to side at the rows of students seated. Some were neatly dressed and friendly-looking, while others were not so well dressed nor as inviting. I supposed that there would still be some nasties, even at a school like Lumiere. I continued to walk down the aisle as a voice called out my name.

I looked toward the back of the bus. It was Simon, the guy I'd met at auditions. "Come on Michael, squeeze through." It felt pretty awesome that someone was calling for me, and it felt more comforting knowing someone on the bus. I squeezed my way through the riff raff and walked up to where Simon was sitting.

"Hey man, how've you been?" He asked as he grabbed my hand and pulled me in, patting me on the back.

"I've been well, thanks Simon. You?" I asked him.

"Yeah, really well, thanks. So you got in! How cool is that?"

"Yes, pretty cool."

"I wasn't sure you liked me that day. When I came out of my examination, I said goodbye and you kind of just stared at me," he said. I thought for a moment, but I didn't remember it. All I remembered was Simon going in, that fuzz, and then heading in myself.

"Yeah, sorry about that. I was just in a kind of daze."

"I get that, man. It was all pretty tense, not knowing if we'd get in or not." As the bus took off, we talked about our audition experience and what we'd done since then. He shared the same love for Andrew Lloyd Weber that I did. Once the bus reached the school, we got off and walked up the stairs which I had tripped on that very first day. Looking back up at the top of the building, I smiled. This was where I was meant to be.

Simon and I walked to the front doors, where we had been instructed in our letter of acceptance to meet, and in front of the doors were other students, all of different builds and appearances. We stood and looked around, then saw two other guys approaching who were from our auditions too. They walked up to us with big smiles of comfort while they waved and said hello. I had the feeling I wasn't the only one glad to know other people there.

The bell rang. It was loud and dominating, much louder than the one in primary school. It felt as though it echoed through the walls and windows. Ms Martinovich, the Dean of Arts, approached and greeted us all. This day she wore a similar suit to the one I remember at auditions, but this one was patterned with black and white zigzags.

"Good morning to you all. If I can have each and every one of your attention for a moment, and I will have you all off to your assigned classes soon." As she spoke, a few other teachers joined her with piles of papers in their hands - two of which were Miss Fitz and Mrs Cornel. "Firstly, I'd like to congratulate you all on your acceptance to this school, and have you know that we are pleased with this year's selections. Even those of you who were late applicants. Among you all are some bright and talented young performing artists who have the opportunity to go far in the courses which you have each been accepted for, being Musical Theatre, Music, Drama and Dance. You know which one is yours. Although you were selected for one particular course, you will have the opportunity to dabble in other classes as electives in semester two. I'd like you to know each choice in life is your own, and what you decide to do in high school can have great impacts on what you do later in life. So please allow our teachers to guide and assist you. Now Miss Fitz and Mrs Cornel here are going to go around and hand each of you your timetable. If you hear your name, please place your hand up in the air and you will be given yours. It will take some time to get used to these grounds, but once you get the hang of it you will soon roam the school like I'm sure you did at your former one. If any of you have any concerns or questions, student services is directly to your left upon entering the double doors of the building, and they are there to help you in any which way they can. If you feel like being a Prima Donna, the doors are not open to you, so please leave the school immediately. There is no room here at Lumiere for them, and I certainly hope that none of you lower yourselves to that standard. This is a place of learning, and I expect you all to do so in a gracious manner. Now, if you will, please listen out for your name and head on to your first class. Once again, welcome to Lumiere and I look forward to getting to know you all much better at a later date." Ms Martinovich had spoken so well and properly. Her posture was perfect and her tone was firm. She was a woman of strength. Again, I couldn't help but feel Mrs Cornel's eyes drawn to me frequently. But I was likely just back in my own head.

*

Making it through my first day, I caught the bus home and met mum in the car park opposite the stop which she had dropped me at. Walking up to the car, she got out and ran to hug me. We got back in to the car where I raved and ranted to her about my day on the way home, and explained to her how I'd met the guys from the audition. As I spoke to her, I could see the delight in her eyes that her son was happy. And I was truly happy. Making friends had been difficult, knowing who to talk to and who not to, but it was such an adventure, and I had loved every second of it.

*

The next day I met Simon at the main station, and we greeted each other with what now seemed to be our thing; grabbing hands to pull each other in and tap one another on the back. When I grabbed his hand and he pulled me in, I rather liked it, although I think I liked it a little more than he did or had intended. However, his hold was strong and meaningful. I still didn't say anything about it to him. It may have been possible that being the first form of not necessarily intimacy, but connection, that I had with someone, that I was looking too far into it. Not to mention that I had never kissed a girl, let alone needing to start thinking about if I had feelings for boys. I did have crushes on girls in primary school, but I had just never spoke to them and, even if I had, I doubt anything would have eventuated.

But, all things aside, I was starting to consider Simon a friend, and wasn't going to do anything to jeopardise that. But the feeling did confuse me, and certainly got me thinking.

Once we got to school, Simon and I met up with the other guys from the initial audition. We were all looking forward to the start of the day, as we had only taken generic classes the previous day, and our first class was Musical Theatre. The bell rang and we all walked to together. Getting to room 106 again sprung a motion of happy feelings within me. Though this time there was a hurdle of girls waiting out the front. Simon, the two other guys and I were the only boys. One of the other guys, Adam, walked over to a girl who screamed his name as they knew each other from outside of school. Simon, the other guy, Andrew, and I stood together and laughed.

"Looks like Adam's got a girlfriend," Simon said.

"Have you got a girlfriend?" Andrew asked Simon.

"Yeah, she goes to another school though. We've been together for two years now," he said. "What about you Michael?"

"Oh no, girlfriend-free," I said awkwardly.

"Ah we'll have to get you one. Look at all them hot bitches over there man," he said, while wrapping his left arm around my neck. I didn't quite know what to say, but luckily Mrs Cornel walked up behind us at that point.

"Hey boys," she whispered between us, then continued to walk to room 106. She unlocked the door with her key and pushed it open. "Come on in, guys and girls." The three of us joined on to the back of the line as everyone started walking in. Once we got inside, we all sat on the floor. I looked around at the faces in the classroom. One thing I liked to do was make up peoples life stories while I looked for potential friends, and as a new thought just that second, who I might be attracted to. This feeling I had with Simon and the mention of girlfriends really had me puzzled.

"Good morning," Mrs Cornel addressed us. "This is your Musical Theatre class. We will meet here three times a week. As specialist students, you will get to choose an elective next semester, however, as Musical Theatre Students your fourth day a week will have you rotate between dance, music, and drama each month, with the fourth month continued with me. This course can be tough. You've chosen a mix of all trades but it can be rewarding, and I hope to share in that reward with you." Mrs Cornel continued to discuss what the class was going to be doing for the year and, as she spoke, I continued to look around at the other students. One girl in particular drew my attention. She had short, dark stylish hair with a white streak in her fringe, black eye shadow and a piercing in her nose. She stuck out to me as different, and I liked that. Whether it was attraction or not, I wasn't sure, but I definitely wanted to get to know her.

Our first assignment for Musical Theatre was to split into groups and re-enact a scene from Phantom of the Opera, one of my favourites. The song 'Masquerade' was the selected scene. A scene where the stage is filled with large and magnificent costumes and the characters wear extravagant masks. Being short on boys, we were split into four groups, with each getting one boy. As luck would have it, I was put with the girl that had intrigued me. The other girls in my group were friendly. One of the girls, Candice, had long wavy blonde hair with light hazel eyes. As I got to know Candice she was a typical teen with her mind in the sky away with the fairies but, although a gossip, she did seem to mean well. The next girl, Renae, had mid-length dark brown hair like mine, and her face was full of freckles. At this stage she was quiet, and I was yet to discover the loyal and kind-natured friend that she would become to me. The last girl in our group was Natalie. She had extremely long, straight blonde hair which came down to her hips. Natalie's eyes were a piercing blue, and her skin tone was like a porcelain doll. She held herself well with a sponge and case in her pocket to powder her nose. Within a few months, she was the most popular girl in school. The girl I had been admiring, however, was Aimee. As we all made small talk getting to know each other this day, my eyes kept connecting with hers. Though the second our eyes met I'd look away, but then at moments I'd look at her to find she'd already been looking at me. Her eyes however did not flinch. As part of the class, we were allowed to venture down to the schoolyards and practice our tasks. As the girls walked ahead, Aimee and I talked and got to know each other a little better, strolling behind.

"So where'd you go to school before Lumiere?" Aimee asked.

"Nowhere special. In fact I'd rather forget that part of my life," I said.

"Oh that's a shame. Not such a popular guy there then?"

"No, definitely not," I responded.

"Me neither," she added. As we continued to walk, I felt a little anxiety returning to my body. "Just for the record. I mean, I don't know you yet, but I think you're cute," she said. My anxiety reached sky high. Not knowing what to say I responded back quickly.

"You too" I said as my body tensed and Aimee smirked.

"We better catch up with them," she said.

"Yeah, we better," I agreed. Aimee grabbed my hand and we started to jog back to the group. As she grabbed my hand that feeling of pin pricks took back to my body. But this time the pin pricks were a good feeling. Anxious, but good. The rest of the class was enjoyable, but at moments confusing as I continued to admire this girl and drifted in and out of focus.

As we stepped through different parts of the song, Aimee and I got closer, and I felt rushes of nerves travel through my body. Was it attraction? I was full of uncertainty. I just wasn't sure what it was. She did make me feel good, and I was certainly infatuated with her. But was it, attraction, or just that she like me was different too and had taken a liking to me? A liking I had never experienced before.

At the end of class Aimee wrote her mobile number down on a piece of paper for me. She told me to call her. The bus trip home felt like it took forever, keen to get home and call her, it wasn't going fast enough! I got into the car after greeting mum with another one of her warm hugs, and on the way home I told her about Aimee, and how I had never felt like this before. I left out the part about thinking I may have had feelings for a guy too, but I did say that I wasn't sure about my feelings for Aimee.

"Oh, Michael. My little angel is all grown up!" Mum said as we pulled into the driveway at home. She undid her seatbelt and leaned over to kiss me on the cheek. "If you think you like her, go for it. But there's no rush or timeline on these things, and if it doesn't work out there's nothing lost."

"But what do I do? Do I ask her out? And what then?" I asked.

"Maybe ask her to the movies - see if there's something you would both like to see. I can take you both and drop her home if she needs. A movie is a good conversation starter, so after that you could go to the cafe and get a milkshake or soft drink." Mum had some good advice, and she was really helpful on settling my mind about a few things. But I wasn't comfortable talking to her about my thoughts of being potentially attracted to a guy just yet. It wasn't that I didn't want to, as she really was my best friend. But the fact is that I knew homosexuality was a very controversial topic. I had no idea about my mum's perspective of same sex relations and how it might change her perspective of me. The fact that we were so close really scared me, yet a part of me said not to be so silly. Of course she would accept me for whatever I was, but another part of me didn't want to risk any awkwardness or even the chance that she might disown me. It happened. I just had no idea how she would react, and it wasn't something I was ready to risk. Especially when I was so unsure about it.

When we got home I grabbed the phone and told mum and dad I was making a call. I ran off to my room and pulled out Aimee's number. She didn't answer. I spent the rest of my night wondering what had happened, why she wasn't answering and if I had said something wrong. After dinner, I went to bed and the whole night my mind ran back and forth over my conversation with Aimee, imagining her face, and picturing us together. My mind started to wonder and I began to picture her taking off my shirt, and suddenly found my penis becoming a little firm. I continued to picture her kissing my chest and then undoing my belt as she kneeled in front of me. I started to rub myself in bed, grabbing my balls and clenching what became rock-hard. In my thoughts, I cupped the back of her head with my hand and pulled my penis out from my underwear, placing it in her mouth as she began thrusting her head back and forward over it. As I imagined this, I grabbed my sheets throwing them back and grabbed my pillow. I mounted it and thrust myself back and forward on it. I imagined pulling Aimee up from her knees, throwing her against the wall and ripping her shirt open to suck and lick her nipples as I grabbed her breasts tight. I continued to thrust against my pillow, as I imagined pulling down Aimee's skirt and knickers to push myself inside her. I thrust and thrust until I burst! Then settled down happily and finally relaxed for the night, turning my pillow over and drifting off to sleep.

*

The next day in Musical Theatre class we were able to come up with our own scenes to the score of the Sound of Music. This time, I wasn't put in the same group as Aimee. Once in our groups, my mind fuzzed in and out, and at times the other students asked for my thoughts, but I had no idea of what had just been said. I barely made it through the session, and afterwards approached Aimee.

"Hi," I said, not knowing what else to say.

"Hey. Fun class, yeah?"

"Yeah, I suppose it was a pretty fun class. How've you been?"

"I've been pretty well. Sorry I couldn't take your call last night. Dad was around and he'd have freaked if he knew I was talking to a boy. I really was looking forward to talking with you though."

"That's okay. Hey listen. I, I.." I stuttered.

"What? What's wrong?"

"No, nothing's wrong. I guess I like you. I wondered if you were keen to go out with me?" I asked, pushing through the pop up stutter. Aimee smiled.

"Yeah, I'll go out with you, Michael," she replied. Inside my mind I started jumping with joy, as high as my imagination would let me, right up into the clouds and beyond. But on the outside I kept cool, and smiled back at her.

"That's great. So I suppose I'll be seeing you around," I said.

"I suppose you will". Aimee slowly stepped closer and gave me a small peck on the lips. I was not expecting it, but my body leaned into it. Then she grabbed tight the hair on the back of my head and stuck her tongue into my mouth, and we began to make out. I didn't know what the hell I was doing but I just stuck my tongue right back into hers and let it glide wherever it went. Once we finished, my eyes stayed closed for a moment as she slowly pulled away and released the hair on the back of my head.

"Nice," I said.

"Nice is right, mister. See you later, Michael," she waved and walked off. My first kiss, I was absolutely over the moon. I couldn't believe it. A year before that I didn't have a friend in the world, and that day I had a girlfriend. At least, I thought that must be what she was, having said she'd go out with me.

5 DISTRACTIONS

The first year of Lumiere passed, and I was soon into my second, grade nine. I had gained the most amazing group of friends, and my grades weren't too bad at all. I think being in a positive environment had helped tremendously in my focus and interest. Not only did I get on with my peers, but I really got on with my teachers as well. I was truly in my element. In companion, to what was before.

Aimee and I didn't last. I took her to the movies the weekend following our kiss, and as we sat there she went to hold my hand and I froze like a frozen boxed meal. After kissing her, as a young inexperienced teenager, I just wasn't sure what came next. The following Monday I walked up to her at school and said *hi girlfriend*. She said that she felt a little weird and asked if we could just be friends. Funnily enough, I was fine with it. I had my first kiss checked off the list and I was ready to live a little.

After Aimee ended things, I felt a boost of motivation within me which saw me put a little effort into how I looked each morning. I began adding product to my hair and even bought some cologne. I received two cards on Valentine's Day my first year at Lumiere, and they were from girls in my Musical Theatre class. But I didn't feel any attraction and didn't pursue them.

Towards the end of grade nine I had really settled in and was really enjoying life. Each morning I'd get to the main station, meet up with Adam and Andrew, who had become my best friends, as Simon had made a new circle of friends with the drama students and hung with that crew more regularly. He still said hi to us occasionally, and there were no hard feelings, but he did drift from us and became more of a popular figure. Andrew, Adam and I had adopted Renae and Candice as friends, and as a group we spent many weekends at each other's places watching movies and eating junk food. I had truly started to appreciate life.

During grade ten, our group became stronger and I had started to develop feelings for Adam. We spent so much time together. Almost each time he looked at me I pictured walking up to him, grabbing hold of the back of his neck and pulling him in to begin passionately kissing him, gliding along his tongue with mine. He was so pretty. Adam had mysterious green eyes which reminded me of the rainforest, and soft thin straight hair with a fringe which sat just to the side of his face. His skin was tanned and smooth, and his smile was simply irresistible. These thoughts in mind, and my lack of interest for girls since Aimee, I felt pretty certain I was gay.

One evening after school, mum picked me up from the bus station and in the car on the way home I approached the topic subtly, asking what she would say if I came home one day and said I had a boyfriend. Mum didn't answer straight away, but it was not an awkward silence, more a silence of thought.

"I'd ask what his name was," she said. Shocked at her response, I tensed up and didn't say anything else to give her an inkling that I might be gay myself. "Why's that, Michael? Do you have a boyfriend?"

"No," I said, and I wasn't lying, I just wasn't filling her in on the details. "I was just curious is all." We continued to drive home, and mum didn't mention anything else about it. Though looking back now, it wasn't subtle, and I'm sure she would have suspected my sexuality in her own mind.

*

After dinner that night, I went to my room to study but it became near on impossible. The second I put pen to paper, my mind would wonder to the image of Adam's face. So handsome, so good-looking and so very pretty, I wanted him, but didn't know how to approach it. I didn't even know if he was gay, although he did share with me once that he'd never had a girlfriend. It did seem a strange thing, being such a pretty boy. Procrastinating, I opened up my laptop and happened to see that he was online. I opened a messenger tab with his address.

"Hi Adam," I typed.

"Hey Michael. How are you?"

"Fine. Just finished dinner."

"Me too... Now to study."

I sat there for a few moments, really puzzled how to continue the conversation.

"Are you free this weekend?" I typed.

"Yes I am. Why's that, Mikey?"

"I just wondered if you might like to come over for the night this weekend?"

"Sounds like a plan. I'll add Andrew to the convo and see if he's free!" Adam typed. It wasn't what I had planned on, but I guess it would be an easy start to making things happen, especially if Andrew wasn't available.

I could suggest that we still get together, just the two of us.

"Hi guys," typed Andrew. Both Adam and I greeted him.

"So Michael's invited us over on the weekend. Are you free?"

"Sweet. I'm there! I'll get my brother to grab us a bottle of vodka," Andrew typed. He had an older brother who Andrew often used to get alcohol. We never drank too much, but enough to share some good times.

*

A week of school passed, and each and every second of it was torment. How did my excitement and thoughts turn from Musical Theatre and my life at Lumiere, to sticking my tongue down a boy's throat within three years? I still loved school, but all my mind could think of was Adam. I wondered how soft his lips would be when they touched mine, and how his body would feel as it rubbed against me. When that final bell rang on Friday, I let out a huge sigh of relief. Andrew, Adam and I all met out the front of the building.

"Hey guys. Let's do this!" I said, as if we were a few guys about to hit the town. We caught the bus to the main station, and then the bus which took us to where mum was waiting. We all got in the car, where I sat in the front next to mum and Andrew got in to be in the back with Adam.

"Hi boys," Mum said.

"Hey Marie," said Andrew and Adam at the same time.

"So, are you boys going to set fire to the suburbs tonight?" Mum asked jokingly.

"You know us, Marie - always the rebels," said Andrew.

Mum laughed, and then she asked about our days while she drove. I observed mum interacting with the guys for a moment, and thought back to when I asked her what she'd say if I had a boyfriend. I just wasn't sure if things would stay this relaxed if I told her I was gay. But I was glad she was social with my friends, and she always made the effort to make them feel welcome and at ease.

Once we got home, we piled out of the car and went inside. As teenagers do, we ran off to my bedroom, put some music on and started talking. We were called for dinner an hour or so after. Gathered at the table sat mum, dad, Luke, Adam, Andrew and me.

"So what's been happening boys?" Dad asked.

"Not too much, I'm sure Michael's told you we're studying the score of Oliver Twist at the moment," Adam replied.

"Yeah, we like playin the old Londonas too don't we?!" said Andrew in a shifty attempt at a British accent. Dad and Mum laughed. Luke sat at the table picking at his food with a fork.

"Do any of you boys have a girlfriend yet or what?" Dad asked. I looked down at my food and gulped. My thighs and arms starting to tense. Dad was another reason I was yet to come out as gay. Being an army soldier, a manly man, I was very hesitant to find out what his response to it would be.

"Oh Cliff, there's not any good ones at our school," said Andrew, and dad laughed.

"What about you, Adam? Anyone there that interests you?" Dad asked, continuing the conversation.

"Not so much, I just haven't really found anyone I fancy," he said. Inside my mind, hidden from the table, I smiled.

"We just can't believe how picky Michael is! All these cards he gets for Valentines Day and not one girlfriend yet. The day he says yes... that girl better be the best god damn looking thing," said dad.

"Clifford!" Mum nudged dad.

"Hey, I'm just saying. The boy's picky," dad remarked.

"Amen to that," said Andrew. Andrew was a funny guy, with little care for the bigger things in life. He was very content to live life day by day and went about his business casually. I was sure he was completely oblivious to my sexual curiosity, but I had a little suspicion that Adam may have suspected something. Sitting across from me at the table, I looked up at Adam eating dinner. Even while he was eating, he looked so god damn pretty. A shy guy, Adam kept on the down-low socially, but really opened up eventually to those he befriended. We had certainly become close over the years, and I dropped some subtleties in remarks I made now and then. However, I was not a hundred per cent sure on his sexual preference and how he felt about me, if he felt anything at all other than being a friend. The move was bold, but I decided to go for it. I moved my leg forward and rubbed it up against his. The table shook as he jumped and pulled his leg back away from mine.

"Adam. Are you okay mate?" Dad asked. Adam looked at me, and then at dad.

"Yeah, no, yes. I, uh, just need to use the bathroom," Adam replied. I remember thinking, *what have I done?* I felt like the rest of the night was now set to be awful and awkward. And once he returned to the dinner table, he didn't make eye contact, nor did he return my move.

After dinner, Adam was very silent. He usually was a quieter guy, but this felt eerily silent. Andrew kept things from feeling too awkward, and we spent the night sitting on the mattresses mum had set out on my bedroom floor for us with the bottle of vodka which Andrew had scored for us. Later in the night, we had polished off the bottle, and began to tell scary stories in the dark. Mid-story, I felt a hand touch my knee.

"Michael?" Andrew said.

"Yes?" I responded.

"You all right?"

"Yeah, fine."

"Why'd you stop the story?" Before I answered, I could feel Adam's thumb rubbing over the top of my knee back and forth.

"I'm not feeling too well, actually. Sorry, guys. Can we re-intervene in the morning?" I asked.

"But now I'll never get to find out what happens to old Peggy Lane," Andrew joked. "But if you insist, I call dibs on Michael's bed!" I smiled, knowing very well that would leave me with the mattress on the floor next to Adam.

"Go for it!" I said. I heard Andrew jump up onto my bed, and adjust himself to get comfortable.

"Good night," I said, laying down conveniently by Adam. For a little while, it was silence and nothing happened. But after a few minutes, I felt Adam's arm reach up onto my waist, again rubbing his thumb back and forth. I then turned on my side towards him, edging in a little closer, as did he. I could feel the warm air from his breath on my face. I edged in a little more, and our bodies touched up against each other. I was stiff solid for a moment, a repeat of the first year when I went to the movies with Aimee, not knowing what came next. I took a deep breath in through my nostrils, which had become a great calming tool for me, and then exhaled.

"Are you okay?" Adam whispered.

"Yeah. Just a little nervous." I whispered back.

"Don't worry, me too" he said. Instinct told me to place my arm around the back of his body, pushing him closer still. I then gently held the back of his neck as our chests caressed against each other. Our noses touched, and I could feel his lips were close. Our breathing began to get heavier.

"I didn't mean to act shocked at dinner. I wasn't."

"What was it then?"

"I don't know about myself, I just didn't want your family to notice, was all."

"That's okay. No-one will notice now," I whispered. We laid there for a few minutes. Our bodies rubbed against each other. I could feel he had formed a boner as it hardened against me, and I'm sure he could feel mine against him. It seemed as if we could not get close enough. Our caressing became stronger and, not able to contain myself any longer, I raised my hand to the back of his head and leaned in to kiss him. His tongue slid into my mouth, and mine into his. Our tongues ran up and down each others, caressing, rubbing and sliding around as our lips connected. It was a moment I can only describe as true ecstasy. Complete darkness and complete silence, but so close and intimate.

We didn't do anything sexual other than kiss. But we kissed aggressively, and it was incredible. I felt more alive than I ever had. The energy pulsing through my body was pure, beautiful and unlike any I'd felt before. When we finally stopped kissing, Adam rolled around and I held him from behind in my arms for the night. When the sun rose, I opened my eyes, staring at the back of Adam's head. I brought my hand up and stroked his soft hair. Adam turned around and looked at me with squinting eyes.

"Good morning," he said. I smiled a smile I had never smiled before.

"Good morning," I replied. He closed his eyes, still turned to me, and I looked at him for a few minutes longer. I heard rustling of the sheets above, and remembered Andrew was still in the room with us. At that moment, Adam rolled back over quickly and I rolled away too. Nerves kicked in, and the passion of the night was suddenly gone. The moment had been ruined.

"Morning boys," Andrew said, as he stretched out his arms and yawned. "No spooning last night I hope, lads," he laughed. I almost laughed myself, but held my tongue and threw my pillow up at him. It was a night that came and went so fast. The rest of the morning was horrible, as Adam and I could not embrace or talk about what had happened between us. We walked out to the kitchen where mum had set up a breakfast bar for us with juices and cereals. I glanced at Adam but he looked away. I wondered if he had regretted the night, but had no way of communicating with him. Shortly after we walked in to the kitchen, mum walked in too.

"Good morning, boys. How was your night? Not too late, I hope," said mum.

"Nah, Michael wasn't feeling the best so we decided not to burn down the suburbs," Andrew replied. Mum walked up and put her arm around me, looking up and grabbing my chin as I was now taller than her.

"That's no good, sweetie. Feeling okay this morning?" I smiled and nodded. "That's good. By the way, Adam, your mum called a little while ago. She has to come pick you up earlier than she thought because your dad needs the car today, so make sure your things are packed." This made me sad. Adam was going to leave with last night's venture unresolved.

When Adam's mum collected him, he didn't even hug me goodbye. He just said thanks and with that was gone. Andrew stayed on a while longer, and he could tell that I was feeling low.

"Should we go for a walk, man?" Andrew asked.

"Yeah, sure," I said. We went out for a slow walk in the fresh air, and with that, I felt the need to open up. He was the next closest thing I had to a best friend other than my mum, and that was good enough for me.

"Andrew, I've got something to tell you," I said, wondering if I was going to ruin two friendships in one day. Andrew didn't say anything, but listened. "Andrew, I think I'm gay. I like guys," I said. He smiled, shook his head and looked down to the ground then up to the sky giggling.

"Oh, Michael," he said, looking over at me. He stopped walking and grabbed my shoulders. "I've known you were gay before you did." I was gob-smacked. He knew. What's more is that he wasn't treating me any different and we just continued to walk and talk. "It's nothing to be ashamed of, man."

"You knew?" I clarified.

"All along," he said.

"Why didn't you ever say anything?" I asked.

"It was kind of something you needed to come to terms with yourself, man. But I'm glad you've told me. And, just so you know, I'm okay with it," he said, comforting me as he put his hand on my shoulder. "And I knew there was something going on with you and Adam last night you cheeky bastard. Why do you think I jumped onto your bed so fast?"Again, I was shocked.

"You knew I liked Adam?" I asked, surprised.

"You weren't the best at hiding it!"

"Do you think my parents know?" I asked.

"No, they're none the wiser. But you are going to tell them, aren't you? Don't hide who you are Mikey." I was so pleased he was okay with it, and I explained my thoughts on mum and dad. He respected my feelings and didn't push it. I was relieved I now had someone I could confide in.

*

The following Monday morning at school was the worst. Adam had not been returning my calls or answering my messages. I caught the bus to the main station that morning almost in tears. I remember thinking, *could I be heartbroken without even having dated the guy?* Mum knew I was feeling down, as she had asked me if everything was all right in the car on the way to the bus stop. I told her I was just a little tired from the weekend, and she seemed to have bought that. When I got to the main station I started looking for Adam immediately. I couldn't find him. I did meet up with Andrew though, and we got on the bus to school together. Having told Andrew about the experience with Adam, he tried to take my mind off of things, and reassured me that it would blow over or even that Adam may have had just been initially freaked out by what he did but possibly cooled down having time to sleep on it. I wasn't so sure though, but appreciated his sentiment.

We got to school but, being a Monday did not have Musical Theatre class, and those first few classes were torture. Every time I looked up at the clock, it was as if the hands on the clock were not moving at all! However, when the bell finally rang, I was uncertain if I wanted to find Adam straight away. *What was he going to do? What was he going to say? What if everything was okay and he wanted to be together - was I ready for that?* Any which way, I walked out from class and over to the year 10 courtyard to where our group always sat for recess and lunch. I looked ahead and Adam was there. I caught his eye as I approached and smiled, picking up my pace. He did not smile, and instead looked away, said something to a girl by his side and then walked off with her. My heart sank. It felt as if it had dropped to the ground, sizzled through, and disappeared into central earth. Beyond, even.

"Hey Michael," Renae said.

"Hey," I responded with little enthusiasm and walked away. Ahead, I saw Andrew walking towards the group. He then started to walk towards me and asked if I was okay.

"Walk with me?" I asked, and he did.

We walked over to the school oval together. I needed to be in an open space with fresh air. We strolled along the outer line around the oval, and we talked.

"That's it, Andrew. He hates me," I said.

"Michael, he doesn't hate you. He's just very confused right now," Andrew said comfortingly. I shook my head and took a deep breath in.

"No, he hates me. I walked towards him and he walked right away."

"Michael, you have to understand that he was probably

experimenting the other night. Perhaps he is disgusted in himself," said Andrew. It made sense. It did seem as though Adam had made the move with his hand on my knee rather confidently after shying away under the dinner table, and it *was* after polishing off a bottle of vodka between the three of us. But it didn't matter to me. I had invested so much thought and so much energy into Adam, so I was naturally upset.

*

He never did talk to me again, he even parted from our group. People do say you don't know what goes on behind closed doors, and perhaps Adam was just not in a position to lead that kind of lifestyle. Pushed his feelings aside. Whatever it was, he had cut me from his life completely. The start to my senior years went downhill from there, and I fell into a state of depression.

I started seeing a school psychologist again, and Andrew and I hit alcohol pretty hard. We were out most weekends at house parties and hosted our own at his place. Our parties were the greatest, as his folks had a few acres of land out in the sticks and would put on bonfires for us. Some of the best memories of my teens. That said, I recall sitting in front of many a bonfire with a beer in my hand, while contemplating jumping in to burn away the pain. The parties were great. But outside of that, started to feel not so much. I never did jump in, I just sat there as the flames flickered in front of me. I kicked on. It's a funny thing, depression. When you're doing what you want to, you can feel on top of the world, but anything and everything else is the greatest de-motivation to keep living. Every ounce of life, responsibility or opportunity presented or delivered to you without your will to take on, seems like the greatest effort of all the tasks and activities on earth. Even pouring milk into your bowl of cereal. Even opening your eyes in the morning. We did have some great times though, Andrew and I. He honestly just had a way to keep me going, never passing judgment, expectations or demands on me. Just sharing experiences, getting drunk and partying. Every party we hit, we ran wild.

To this moment Andrew remains my best buddy. I'll miss him. I wonder, if I go through with this tonight, if he'll visit me in prison? If he'll still pass no judgement, once these hands of mine have been covered with blood.

6 HONORABLE INDIVIDUALS

Sat in the Dean of Arts' office around Ms Martinovich's desk were Mr Culver, Mr Stanley, Miss Fritz and Mrs Cornel. I was the topic of conversation. I didn't want to be part of the Musical Theatre course anymore. I had lost the passion, my spark of interest in it, and truth be told I just didn't care anymore. Looking back, it's profound what an impact Adam's rejection had on me. Although, it wasn't *just* rejection was it? They'd cut me from their life, tossed me aside like a piece of expired meat. It made me feel worthless. It made me feel disposable. I started to sob as I opened up and explained my feelings to the panel of teachers.

"I just can't cope anymore," I said, as tears built up in my eyes. "Musical Theatre was my love, but I cannot sit in that classroom anymore. I feel a huge void that cannot be filled. I understand that it may sound stupid to you, but I come from a background of nothing. Not a friend in the world." As I continued, the tears started to roll from out of my eyes, down my cheeks and to the floor. "The first year I started here, I was overwhelmed with happiness. Each of you granted me the greatest gift I have ever received by allowing me to attend this school and, as the years went by, I felt more and more part of something and thought I had found my place. But things changed last year." I started to rub the tears from my eyes, and they started to swell. I sniffed as my nose began to run. "I don't expect you to completely understand, but there's something I just cannot deal with in that space anymore. I'm not myself anymore, or at least I don't know the person I've become. It's hard for me to find the motivation or love for anything at all right now. I know you've noticed."

I felt as though my excuses were petty, but I couldn't explain the full story, not being able to handle being in the same room as Adam – without *outing* myself. I just couldn't sit in a room with a guy who tore my heart out, not for one more day. Adam had become a trigger, and I needed to remove it from my life in order to move on. The second I walked into that space and saw Adam, every part of my body that held strength and optimism fell dead, and my anxiety came rushing back. My psychologist said that my feelings linked back to when I was rejected in primary school, but I believed I was just dealing with a fucked-up situation.

"Before you go on, Michael," interrupted Mr Culver, "I told you the very day that you auditioned for us that we were concerned, and that you would have to pull your weight." He seemed stern. I could feel the word 'expelled' coming on, and I leant over my knees and burst into tears. Mr Culver paused for a moment. Ms Fitz stood, pulled a tissue from the box on Ms Martinovich's desk and handed it to me while putting her other hand out towards Mr Culver gesturing to quieten him. She knelt by my side and placed her fingers under my chin.

"Chin up, Michael. We're all here," she said, looking over her glasses. "None of us are angry. Just hear the man out." She stood and returned to her seat.

"As I was saying, Michael," Mr Culver started to speak again, "we told you to pull your weight. And you certainly have." I looked up at him and he smiled at me. "Your grades improved dramatically in your first few years here, Michael, and we're proud of you."

"It has been the inaction of those who could have acted," said Mrs Cornel. "That is what I said to you when you first appeared in room 106. And right now, you have acted." I sat back up, and my tears began to dry. Mrs Cornel walked up to me, knelt down and leaned her arm on my knee. "You've done a real gutsy thing coming to us, Michael. Some kids cannot hack it and they drop out. We've lost students to suicide because they couldn't take whatever issues they were dealing with on top of this course, but you know what Michael? All they had to do was act on what they felt," she said. "I stood up and welcomed you to this school, and I'll be damned if I don't see you graduate from it." I could not believe the support. I smiled gratefully. Mrs Cornel had really spoken her words with passion. Perhaps the times I'd thought she'd taken notice of me, she'd seen a little of herself, in me.

"Michael," Mr Stanley began to speak, "I've been there - right in those shoes of yours. When Mrs Cornel says you're gutsy, she means it." Mr Stanley looked at me from across the room with a stare of admiration, while pointing his pen at me with precision as he continued to speak. "The important thing here is that we make you feel better about yourself. If you ever need anything, come and see me."

"Thank you. Thanks to you all," I said, starting to swell up with tears again, but this time of gratitude. Mrs Cornel hugged me. Ms Martinovich sat at her desk and explained to me that she would pull me out of the Musical Theatre course, but I would continue as a regular student at the school. If any students were to ask my whereabouts in Musical Theatre, I was instructed to say I had been selected for a senior music historical course. It was a non-existent class, but they put the title in place for me.

"Actually, Mrs Cornel," Ms Martinovich said. "I think you should make an announcement in class, don't you?" Ms Martinovich smirked, and Mrs Cornel looked back at me.

"I think that's a mighty fine idea," said Mrs Cornel.

I looked at each of the teachers around me, not seeing them as teachers any more, but as honorable individuals.

*

Back at home, lying on my bed while looking up at the ceiling, I wondered about my life, its future and purpose. I had entered Lumiere so excited and full of enthusiasm, yet somehow my distractions led to a lack of enjoyment for anything again. *How could one boy have such an impact on me?* Most nights since he cut me from his life I had come home and cried. But as I was relieved from the Musical Theatre course, I felt stronger and stronger each term that passed by. But the break between grade ten and eleven saw me spiral, without having school to throw myself into, it was a real waste. I found myself fall back quickly into partying and drinking, filling the void of now both the lack of a boy and a passion in my life, but what had I really gotten out of it? The anxiety that built inside me leading up to my return to school was astronomical – although I tried to convince myself otherwise at the time. Thankfully, Andrew had stuck by my side. In fact the nights we went out drinking he would have me question if I needed another – no matter how ignorant of an attitude I adopted to such questions. He visited regularly, and I could always count on him to cheer me up. The parties he dragged me out to were fun, I'll admit it. And I spent a lot of time being a 'kiss slut' as he called it, making out with randoms who showed interest. I guess I was trying to fill the void, but nothing ever did. No matter what the events, I always ended up the same; home alone, feeling like I had a gaping hole inside my chest.

*

The year went on, and I was now seeing my psychologist on a weekly basis. She talked to me about my feelings, how I coped with situations and why I thought I felt the way I did. I shared with her how I had invested so much hope into Adam, and how magical the one night we had together had been. I continued to describe the feelings and emotions I had experienced the next day, and how once he left he hadn't spoken a word to me again. All she could give me was scenarios of why I might feel the way I did, but my mind wasn't really present when she spoke most of the time. I just wanted a magic pill to make me better. The group of friends I had made in my lower years were still friends with me, but when I was around them I felt alone and disengaged, as if anything I contributed to the conversation was just momentary and didn't matter seconds later. I also wondered continuously how many of my peers I'd actually continue to see after high school, and for the ones I might not, if it was worth investing time in them at all. The only person I spoke with genuinely was Andrew, and I was thankful to have him as my friend. I wasn't attracted to him in any way, and

I was okay with having just the one friend, because he was a true one. My best one.

*

A day arrived that I had been dreading, the day that mum came to school to see my psychologist with me. I had been dreading it, because I wasn't looking forward to what mum might feel, knowing her son was depressed. But in a way, I felt she knew already. Our happy greetings and farewells in the car had become silent as I lost enthusiasm to please her as I once had. I just couldn't be bothered trying anymore. My hugs became less sincere, and I couldn't remember the last time I got into the car with an exciting story to tell her. Or even, a smile on my face.

Out the front of school, I held a yellow slip which excused me from class to meet mum. Looking over the stairs which I so excitingly walked up and tripped once upon a time, I saw mum approaching. It took every bit of energy I had to force a smile as she came closer, and she greeted me with one of her warm hugs, not that I felt its warmth that day. She followed beside me as we walked to the psychologist's office, and when we got there she looked at me with a sadness in her eyes, but continued to smile as if to hide any hurting she was feeling at that time. Virginia, the school psychologist, opened the door. She was an older lady, with ocean blue eyes, short grey hair and an old knitted cardigan which she had draped over her shoulders.

"Come in," she said.

Mum and I walked into Virginia's office together, where there were two chairs set side by side. "Take a seat," she said, gesturing to them before closing the door. Mum and I each took a seat, and you could have cut the silence with a knife. Virginia sat down in front of us on her office chair by her desk. The office was small, dated and aged, much like the rest of the school. The furniture was covered in imitation dark brown wood looking grain, and her desk had a hard yellow laminate bench top. Not the most inviting of an environment, but Virginia managed to set a comforting atmosphere to the space. "Hi, Marie. I'm Virginia," she introduced herself as she held her onto her cardigan with one hand and shook my mum's hand with the other. "I'd just like to open today's session by saying that Michael and I have spoken now for some time, and I felt it was best we brought you in here today. Initially Michael felt very protective of you and your feelings, but most recently we've agreed it's best for his health that you come in and know what's been going on with him. That some transparency is brought into the family home."

Mum nodded and looked over at me, the sadness in her eyes was now joined by concern. She leant over to grab my hand and held it tightly as she looked back at Virginia.

"So what's been going on?" Mum asked. Virginia looked at me.

"Would you like to start, Michael?" she asked. I took a deep breath in, inhaling through my nose and exhaling out my mouth.

"Mum," I began, feeling the tension and emotions start to gather in my chest. "I haven't been too happy." But before I could continue, my tears built as the emotions within my body took over. Combined with my own pity and the realisation that mum was about to hear her son was severely depressed, my tears began to stream. Mum's eyes became glassy, and she leant over to hold both my hands as I sat in a puddle of tears. Mum looked back to Virginia as she stepped back into the conversation to pick up where I had stopped.

"Michael hasn't been happy. But he is adamant you should know it has nothing to do with you or his father, and that he loves you both very much." Mum began to cry herself.

"I knew something was wrong, Virginia. He just hasn't been himself lately. It's been going on for a few months now, and it was tearing me apart not knowing why. Hearing it now is really hitting home," said mum.

Virginia passed us both a tissue box. Mum took it and placed it on her lap, taking a tissue to give to me and then one for herself. Mum let go of my other hand and began to rub my back.

I didn't discuss my interest in boys that day. Virginia had said prior to the session that it was up to me to tell her about that in my own time, and that the immediate issue was sharing how I felt with mum so that I had support at home. Although it was initially hard, talking with mum and Virginia helped. It felt as if a weight had been lifted off of my chest. The session was helpful in reconnecting with mum, and I remember feeling that I should have done it much sooner.

*

The weeks that followed saw mum and I rekindle our relationship and, although I wasn't completely happy, the hole inside my chest didn't feel as large a gap. Knowing that mum was by my side, having supporting teachers at school, and having Andrew as my best friend, I felt lucky. The teachers had cared enough to help me through a rough time and, although my dad was not always present, he took care of me, kept a roof over my head and had never shown me anything but pride and love. I also had a mother who held absolute unconditional love for me and, although I had decided to wait until I had my first boyfriend, I was ready to tell her who I was. It's funny now to think, that all I had to do was open up to those around me, sharing how I felt and what I was going through, in order to let go of all the anxiety. I had been carrying so much baggage, trying to battle on myself, with no real support system in place. Once that support system was established, things started to pick right back up.

If only I held that same support system today.

7 CAMERON

My final senior year arrived, having thoroughly enjoyed the Christmas break. Now openly communicating with mum and supported by my teachers and my bestest buddy in the world, Andrew. I felt somewhat okay. I had also opened up to a few of my peers at school, as after opening up with mum I felt closing myself off to them wasn't helping me at all. It actually felt nice to open up. All of a sudden I had a huge support network of people surrounding me, and life wasn't so bad. The only person in my life I was beginning to feel a little disconnected from was my dad and, although I knew he loved me as his son, I never felt able to talk with him casually. My brother, Luke, was a boy's boy and I was not, which is why I felt he and dad always clicked so well. While mum and I clicked in our own special way, I wouldn't say either of them favoured Luke or I, but they certainly connected with each of us in different ways. Sat at my dresser and looking back at the situation now, it was so clear, with what I had just gone through, that all I had to do was open up about who I was. However, at the time, I held a front around dad. It was some kind of macho man guard that I put up when he was around. All I really needed to do was let that guard down. But it's easier to look back and think these things, isn't it?

In my final year at school, hype was building as the Senior Ball approached and everyone planned their futures. Friends in our group had plans to go to university to get their bachelor in arts, while others were interested in studying another area of the arts at TAFE – Technical and Further Education. Some were keen to travel, and Andrew had decided he didn't want to pursue a career in theatre. He was looking at becoming an apprentice to get a trade. I, however, wasn't sure what I wanted to do. Not being the most academically gifted, university really wasn't an option for me, and I didn't fancy the idea of continuing study at TAFE. Rather than worrying about my future, I decided to just embrace my final year at school, try to enjoy life, and focus on my immediate general wellbeing. It had been a pretty rough journey to this point after all.

Earlier in the year, I signed up to a social media site where my curiosity found me browsing profiles of local gay males. There were a few younger profiles which I requested to connect with, and there were a few which started sending me requests once I had joined. As I wasn't 'out' to my friends, with the exception of Andrew, I privatised my profile. I set my sexuality to gay - allowing my profile to come up in any other gay male searches in the area - but my privacy setting meant that it was not visible to any friends or family that I added or whom added me to their accounts.

One Friday afternoon at school the bell rang, signifying the end of the day. I was in a class with Andrew, and he asked what I was up to for the weekend. I told him I was keen to get home because I was scheduled to have a chat with one of the guys I had been talking with, at eight o'clock. He warned me about people who pretend to be someone online that they weren't, and that I should be careful. It was mostly common sense, but he was just assuring I was being careful.

"Who stays at home talking on messenger on a Friday night, anyway?" Andrew asked.

"Andrew, this guy and I really click. I love that you're looking out for me, but Cameron and I just have this connection," I explained.

"Cameron? He sounds like a douche," joked Andrew.

"Shut your face!"

"I suppose I'll leave you to it," said Andrew, and he waved as we walked our separate ways. I got onto the bus, with the congestion of students around me, and sat up by the front in my own little world. All I could think of was getting home to speak with Cameron. Our conversations were deep - he too had experienced a brutal primary school life and had in fact encountered worse of a time than I did. A few years older than me, Cameron had opened up to me about the night of his eighteenth birthday party, where it got around to his unsuspecting parents that he was gay. While he was inside with some friends by a window that night, his father came up and pushed him through it. He told him he was no son of his and that he was to pack his bags and never come back. It was horrible, and a further reason I was still hesitant to tell the rest of my friends and parents about myself, as people could truly be unpredictable sometimes.

I got off the bus where mum was waiting for me as usual, smiling and waving. I was so glad that I had managed to fight through my depression and rekindle my relationship with her. There were still some issues I was dealing with, but I was glad mum and I were back on track. I got in the car, embraced one of those warm hugs of hers and sat back to put my seatbelt on.

"What's the plans tonight then, my little angel?" mum asked.

"I've got to finish my homework tonight. I know it's the weekend but I'm on a roll," I said, covering up my intentions of speaking with Cameron.

"That's very responsible of you, Michael. I'm proud of you," she said.

When we got home, mum served a delicious meal, as she did most nights, and as soon as I had finished, I wiped my mouth with a serviette excusing myself from the table.

"All right, guys, I've got to hit the books," I said.

I sat in my room with my laptop open. It was ten minutes to eight o'clock. I was early, but excitedly anxious. Andrew was online.

"Who sits on messenger at 7:50 on a Friday night?" I typed to him.

"Ha ha, very funny," Andrew typed back. "He online?"

"Nah, not yet," I typed. Just at that second, Cameron's address came up online. "Sorry, I lied. He just came on, talk to you later."

"Hi Michael," Cameron typed. I responded straight away. We talked for hours. Each key I pressed down on the keyboard felt like a tally of how emotionally close we were becoming. I looked up at the time and it was almost midnight.

"I love how easily I can speak with you," I typed.

"I know," Cameron replied. "I think we should meet up this weekend..." I read his last message, unsure of what to say. I wasn't sure if I was ready to meet him, but if not now, when?

"I'd like that," I replied without thinking, and before I knew it we were arranging to meet in the city at noon the next day. We planned our meeting spot and said goodnight. I went to bed extremely anxious, but in a new kind of way, with a feeling of butterflies in my stomach. But at that moment my stomach turned. What if this turned out to be another Adam experience, investing so much time and energy only to be cut away? Surely not. Adam was young and confused, whereas this was an older guy who knew who he was and wanted to meet me. What if we went to the movies and I froze up again like I did in the first year of high school with Aimee? As my thoughts swam around my mind, my eyelids began to lower and I drifted off to sleep.

The next morning, I woke at 10.30am. I jumped out of bed having slept longer than I wanted to and rushed into the shower. I washed myself faster than I ever had before, and gelled my hair before getting dressed. Buttoning the last button of my shirt I looked into the mirror and hoped that I was going to be attractive to Cameron. I adjusted my collar, ran a hand over my hair and nodded to myself. I pulled out some cologne, and sprayed it each side of my neck, on my chest, shirt, wrists and back of my head before leaving the house.

*

On the bus I checked my mobile phone – it was 11:15. It took half an hour to reach the city and each minute my buzz buzzed twice as much. I arrived at the central city station at 11:48, and walked briskly through Perth city to the spot where we had agreed to meet. I was used to weekend city hangs with Andrew and knew my way pretty well. It was Perth, after all. There wasn't too many streets to know. Waiting, I saw a guy in black jeans and a black shirt walking my way. He had sunglasses on and a diamond piercing in his left ear which glimmered in the sun. He took his glasses off as he got close and smiled. I recognised him from his profile picture straight away. My feet, calves, knees and thighs tensed. I didn't know what to do, what to say or how to act. I couldn't believe I actually agreed to meet up with him. It was a first for me, meeting up with a stranger from online.

"Hey, Michael," Cameron said as he extended his arms to hug me. I walked into his gesture and embraced in a hug. We parted and looked at each other for a moment. He kept smiling. "So, how are you?" he asked.

"In disbelief that the guy I've been talking with all this time is standing right in front of me," I replied.

"Well, it's me," said Cameron. "Shall we walk?"

"Let's," I replied. We walked to a coffee shop he recommended which he swore served the best iced coffee frappes in Perth, and ordered them to take away. Continuing to walk I swirled the straw in my takeaway cup and sipped what really was the best iced coffee frappe, not that I had anything to compare it to, for it was my first. "Mmm, that's great."

"I told you," he said. For a while we talked about school, and he assured me that once I graduated there was an entire life out there waiting for me that I couldn't even begin to comprehend yet. He said that life after high school becomes your own, and you can make what you want of it. We talked about his work as a personal assistant and, after we finished our frappes, he asked if I'd like to go see a movie.

"Sure," I answered, keen to continue. He took me to an old heritage cinema off of an arcade. It had awesome pictures hung of celebrities, from Barry Humpreys to Nicole Kidman, each in differently styled frames. The cinema had character, and the candy bar was very cute, with the person behind it wearing an old nineteen-twenties candy store service-like uniform. Cameron bought us our tickets and popcorn, and we took our seats at the very back of the cinema. He had led the way.

As the movie started, the lights dimmed and Cameron leant over to me, and whispered in my ear to thank me for coming to meet him. He then grabbed my hand and held onto it. I didn't feel so nervous, in fact I just went with it. He seemed to be leader, and he led me into a place of real comfort. A few minutes into the film, I loosened up completely. As the movie continued, so did Cameron, as his hand made its way onto my thigh. Only a few minutes after putting his hand on my thigh, he grabbed my hand and placed it on his inner thigh. I went with it, and started to rub it with my thumb. Hell, what did I have to loose. He began to rub my thigh too. Then he grabbed my face with his other hand, and turned it to face his. Instantly, he moved himself in and started to make out with me. It was a hot, tense and passionate moment. I became rock hard instantly as he started to rub my crotch. Time crept up on us fast, and the credits ran while the lighting started to fade back up. We disengaged quickly as we realized this. The length of a movie had felt like it was but a second. I had been totally engrossed in Cameron. Then, he turned to me and asked if I wanted to go back to his place.

"All right," I agreed, in a complete daze. Not really knowing what I had just agreed to at the time. We walked out of the cinema, and he said he had to go to the toilet. I quickly pulled my phone out and text mum while he was away to avoid seeming uncool. *Hi mum, I just thought I'd let you know I'm going to be staying at Andrew's place tonight. Love you lots. M xoxo*

Once Cameron came back, he asked if I was ready to go, and upon my response we quickly got on the train and started our journey. What was I thinking? I thought. I had just gotten aboard a train with a guy I barely knew, a stranger really, and I was off to who knows where. My hormones had gotten the better of my logic, I supposed. I had never felt so enthralled before, and I was taking a chance on it. When we were sat in the cinema, rubbing each other's thighs and crotches while we made out, I felt so good. He made me feel so good. I wasn't ready for that feeling to end. *In the closet,* being out in public with another gay guy felt remarkable. Rebellious and intense. I liked it. Come what may.

As we sat beside each other on the train, our legs touched. We subtly moved them against each other, as if to say 'I'm still here, waiting to ravish you'. I was thriving on adrenalin.

"This is our stop," Cameron said, winking at me as he stood up and walked to the door. As the doors opened, I stepped into the unknown, and it was Midland. We walked out and away from the station onto a road. Cameron grabbed my hand and held it. He certainly had a confidence about him, a confidence I could only dream of at the time. I would have usually been inclined to pull away, but something about him provided assuring comfort, and so we walked hand in hand.

We reached the top of a hill, and then walked further still.

"Just a turn away," he said. We walked around the corner and onto his street. He pointed out his place ahead – it looked homely and cared for. The front garden was tastefully maintained, with gorgeous hedges trimmed to line the front window panes. It had a garden bed full of roses either side of a pathway which led to the front door.

"Nice garden," I commented.

"Thanks. It's my mum's, keeps her busy," Cameron said. Hearing that it was his mum's settled my wonder as to if this was his own place or not. In fact, the thought that he lived with his mum, and not alone ruled out the thought *serial-killer*, which has started to become a very real possibility in terms of my thoughts as we walked along the road, and so I relaxed even more. At least, as relaxed as I could be while adrenalin pumped through my veins.

"Is your mum home?" I asked.

"No, she's away visiting relatives at the moment. We've got the place all to ourselves," he said, seductively. My adrenaline pumped sky high. He unlocked the front door and pushed it open, allowing me to enter first.

"Thank you," I said, as I walked inside to the further unknown. I walked down the corridor, with photos of family portraits hung on the walls.

"Is this your father?" I asked, pointing to an older but friendly looking chap.

"Are you joking?" Cameron asked. "Mum wouldn't dare hang a picture of him up in this house, not after what he did to me. That's mums partner, Paul. They met not long after she left dad," he explained, then grabbed hold of my hand again. "Come on then, unless you want to stand around looking at family photos all day?" I laughed awkwardly and shook my head. We walked past the living room and kitchen, down another corridor and then stepped inside his bedroom. He shut the door.

"Just in case," he said. He wandered over to his bed and sat down as I stood awkwardly, while my heart beat a million miles a minute. "Come sit down," he said, and he moved his hand over the bed. I walked over and sat myself down next to him.

"It's okay. You don't need to be nervous," he said, while moving his hand onto my thigh. I shut my eyes and felt his hand begin to rub and squeeze my thigh. It was like before when we were in the cinema, but this time with more passion and drive. My body was riddled with nerves, but it felt so good. I felt myself become firm again – so did he as he grabbed hold of me. "Do you like that?"

"Yeah, that's nice" I answered. I was in a slight state of panic as my heart began to race, clueless of what to do.

"Just relax," he said. As he went to undo my belt, I sat there in silence with my eyes shut. Every touch felt good. Great. Okay, fucking incredible. He slid my pants off and threw them away as I opened my eyes and saw him staring towards me with eyes like a predator ready to pounce. I kind of liked the thought that I might be prey. That he wanted me. I sat there, bulging against my underwear with erotic excitement and exhilaration. Cameron stood up beside the edge of the bed and asked if I wanted to take off his belt. I leant forward and undid it, sliding it out from his jeans. He then pushed me back softly, and took off his jeans. Now that we were both in our underwear, he climbed back onto the bed, grabbed my head and started making out with me. His hand slid beneath my underwear with determination and grabbed my penis without hesitation. He moved me with force to lay across the bed.

He pulled off my shirt, and then took off his own. Tossing them aside quick. Lowering his bare chest down on to mine, he kissed my neck, and then moved down to my pecs. He continued making his way down further, kissing my torso, my belly and then pulled my underwear down, grabbing my now exposed hardened penis, and leaned down placing it in his mouth. He started to suck it, and it felt amazing, like wet slippery bliss as I felt his tongue roll over it. I arched my back and let out a moan. He continued to suck, and moved his tongue up and down my shaft, right up to its tip while I moaned hard trying not to scream. I had never felt or experienced anything so satisfying.

As he continued, my whole body felt overwhelmed. Cameron pulled his lips away and moved back up to meet with mine.

"I want you to fuck me, Michael," he said. I didn't know exactly what I was doing, but I just went with what came naturally. My urges moved me to grab his arse cheeks and spread them, then sliding my fingers around to his front, I grabbed hold of his rock hard dick with urge and eagerness, never having held one other than my own, feeling and experiencing everything in that moment that I could. My fingers wandered below him and started to fondle his balls. Roll them in my hands.

"I'll be back," whispered Cameron, as he got off me and from the bed, heading for a bathroom joined to his room.

I laid on the bed, restraining myself from shouting out to the world that I was about to lose my virginity, and containing myself from running after him and pouncing as a predator myself. When Cameron came back, he brought a condom with him. He got back onto the bed, and sat on-top of my thighs in front of my standing tall salute, sliding the condom on to it with his mouth as he arched over. So tender and new to this, every moment felt unbelievable. New and thrilling. Raw. Cameron sat back up, positioning himself over me and grabbing hold of me so I met the centre of his anus, and he moved down slowly. I cannot describe how inconceivably spectacular it felt as I entered him. He grabbed the back of my legs and bent them in towards us as he leant forward and thrust himself up and down on top of me. I went for it, I started to fuck him. I fucked him and fucked him, sliding in and out of his tight hole clenching around me until I came. I let out the greatest moan of pleasure my body had ever had, and then came to a halt with complete and utter satisfaction. Once we finished, Cameron got up and opened the window while lighting a cigarette. I laid puffed, with all my energy spent. I turned my head to look at him, finding that the sunlight had gone and night was upon us. I had lost my virginity, and I was ecstatic!

That feeling, ecstatic. Sitting at my dresser, as I stare at my motionless self in the mirror, I realise it's a feeling I haven't felt in a very long time now. I wondered what it might feel like to take a knife to that first queens chest. If the first time piecing their body, as I entered them with a sharp blade, might be the same feeling as when I'd first fucked Cameron. When I fucked him and fucked him. I wondered, if at first stab I'd hack away with as much urge and eagerness as when fucking Cameron.

8 VICTOR

The Monday that followed, after fucking Cameron, I was pulsing with positivity. I got off the bus at school and ran to our group's meeting spot. Andrew, Renae and Candice were there. If there was a time to come out to the girls, this was it.

"Morning, gang," I said. Andrew was eating a doughnut and the girls were holding takeaway coffee. They looked up at me and said good morning with bright smiles. "So I've got something to tell you this morning," I said. Andrew looked at me with an inquisitive glance, which I returned with a slight nod and smile as if to suggest all was okay.

"What?" asked Renae.

"Well, I've actually been looking for the right time to tell you for a little while now," I began to explain.

"Is something wrong?" asked Candice.

"No, nothing's wrong, but it's certainly something I'm not sure how you will react to, so I'm just going to say it and whatever happens, happens." I paused for a moment. "I like men." The girls looked at each other and smiled. Renae came up to me and grabbed my hands, holding them between us.

"I'm so happy for you, Michael" she said, embracing me.

"Happy?" I asked.

"That you're okay with it. Candice and I suspected, and I just want you to know that we accept you for who you are," she said. Candice joined us and put her arms around my shoulders. It was a nice feeling, being accepted, which truly made hiding all this time a huge regret, when I could have just been myself from the start.

"Anything else you want to tell us?" Andrew asked.

"Oh yeah, come sit down," I said to Renae and Candice. We all sat. "I met up with a guy I'd been talking to for a while online, and he took me to the movies..."

"Oh, so sweet!" said Renae. Renae and Candice looked keen to know the story, while Andrew did not look as keen.

"Yeah, it was nice. But we didn't really see the movie… we started kissing and our hands wandered for a bit," I said. Renae and Candice looked at each other, then smirked and giggled.

"What happened next?" Renae asked.

"A bit of gobby I imagine, slut," Candice added, laughing as Renae slapped her hand. "What?" she said.

"Michael wouldn't stoop that low on the first date," said Renae.

"Well not so low in public, anyway," I remarked. "He asked if I wanted to go back to his place." Renae's jaw dropped.

"I told you," Candice said, giggling. "Slut!"

"Michael…" Renae said in disappointment.

"I know, I know. But we related so much on the same level and I've been hiding who I am for so long. It felt nice to be with someone who had been through the same things as me when he went to school. When he started kissing me, I was mesmerised," I explained.

"When he went to school? How much older is he?" asked Renae.

"Not too much older, maybe four or five years," I said.

"Slut, slut, slut, slut, slut!" said Candice, laughing hysterically.

"Slut is right. Tell them what else happened, Michael," said Andrew, looking at me unimpressed, as I had already told Andrew what happened over online chat. The girls looked at Andrew.

"You knew?" Renae asked.

"Oh it doesn't matter, just tell us what happened next," said Candice slapping at my belly.

"Well, we got to his place, and it was pretty much into it straight away," I said.

"Into what?" asked Renae.

"Sex, Renae, god damn it," said Candice. Renae looked at me seeking confirmation.

"Is that what happened?" she asked.

"Yeah," I said hesitantly.

"Jesus, Michael. How well did you know this guy? Did you use protection?" asked Renae, concerned.

"Yes, Renae. I used protection," I replied.

"Well, good. Is there more?"

"Well, that's where it gets interesting. We had sex, and he lit a cigarette. Then he said there was a spare bed made up in the room next door, and that he was going to have a shower." The girls looked unimpressed, while Andrew had a look as if to say *I'm not surprised.*

"So what did you do? What happened the next day?" asked Renae.

"I went to bed, in the spare room. I'll admit it was weird but I didn't really care," I said.

"What do you mean? He used you for sex," said Renae.

"Well, that's just it. I kind of felt like I used him for it too. Like when we left the cinemas I knew what was going to happen," I explained further.

"See? I told you! Sluuuuuut!" Candice continued to chant. I giggled with her, but Andrew and Renae stayed disapprovingly silent.

"Well, just don't make a habit of it, Michael," said Renae.

"Oh Renae, take a chill pill," said Candice. "It was his loss of virginity. We've all done that."

"Yeah, but mine was with my boyfriend of seven years, and it wasn't just sex, we made love" said Renae.

"Oh it's just sex Renae!!! You are an exception anyway. Primary school sweethearts are a rarity," said Candice. "Who wants to stay with the one guy when there's a catalogue of them?!"

"Never mind," said Renae, as she stared at me. "I'm just glad you're okay. What happened the next day?"

"I woke up, he gave me a towel, said there was cereal in the pantry if I was hungry, and then walked me back to the station."

"See," said Andrew. "Had that been a weirdo, he would have knocked you over the head and thrown your body into the wastelands." Andrew finished speaking and walked off.

"Andrew!" I called out, as he continued to walk.

"It's okay. He's just concerned. We all are," Renae said.

"I'm not," said Candice, continuing to laugh. Renae gave her a death stare. "What? I'm just saying... You're a slut!" Candice continued, and pushed my shoulder playfully.

"Just be careful, Michael. I'm really proud of you for coming out and all, but I'd hate to see you end up in a gutter or with some kind of sexually transmitted disease. Play it safe," said Renae. I was very thankful to have such a caring and concerned friend. If anything, coming out had brought us closer, even in those last few seconds. In her concern, she'd shown me a level of care that only a true friendship would hold. A genuine one. However, I was still on a high, and I wasn't coming down until I was ready.

The school year carried on as it always did. I had taken Renae's advice about being more careful. I still spoke with guys online, but I hadn't met up with any of them. I'm not sure if it was because we didn't share as much of a connection as Cameron and I had, or whether I was just more wary and the novelty of the first guy I clicked with had worn off. I text Cameron occasionally, but his responses were brief and he never tried to initialise contact. Andrew came around, but he still played devil's advocate, which I appreciated as it kept me grounded.

I asked mum one night if it would be okay for Andrew, Renae and Candice to stay over. She agreed, and so one Saturday afternoon the three of them came over. We took a trip down to the local video store where we picked a few films to watch, along with some crisps, soft drink and chocolate. We set up mattresses on the floor in my room and broke out the junk food. We had become such a great circle of friends, and we thoroughly enjoyed each other's company. I had the laptop switched on beside the mattresses, and a guy I had been talking with appeared online. I started shaking Renae and Candice's legs and pointed to the screen.

"That's the guy, Victor!" I said. I turned on to my stomach on the mattress in front of the laptop and pulled it towards me. The girls gathered around and Andrew sat back eating chips.

Victor was a guy I had been talking to more regularly in-between the others that dropped in and out, and I had filled in Renae, Candice and Andrew about our conversations. He seemed like a nice guy. Unlike some of the seedy men online. Victor just talked with me about his days at work and his own circle of friends and their experiences. I think he enjoyed reminiscing in his past and projecting life lessons on to me. I also like it. He felt a little like a role model – an attractive one.

"What's he said?" asked Renae.

"Nothing yet," I said. "Should I open up the conversation?" I asked.

"Yes, go on," said Renae.

"Hi Victor," I typed. Nothing happened for a few seconds, and then the typing symbol appeared.

"Hi Michael!" Victor responded.

"What are you up to tonight?" I typed back.

"Oh, nothing," he typed in response. "You?"

"I've got a couple of friends over tonight..." I typed, but before I hit send looked at Candice and Renae beside me. "Should I invite him over?" I asked. Renae hesitated, but Candice jumped in to support the idea. Renae looked back at Andrew.

"What do you think, Andrew?" asked Renae.

"Why not? We're all here, aren't we? If anything it'll give Michael a few people to judge his character," Andrew replied, and smiled at me.

"All right, go on," said Renae.

"I've got a couple of friends over tonight... Would you like to join us?" I typed.

"Sure!" Victor typed back instantly. I typed in my address. He said he had a car and could be over in half an hour. I let mum know that another friend was coming, and I'd answer the door when the doorbell rang. Renae and Candice paired like a couple of giddy teenagers, Candice having a bit of an influence over Renae. Andrew kept cautious. The doorbell rang, and I ran past the lounge room where mum and dad were sitting while they watched TV. I placed my hand on the doorknob, took a quick breath in, and opened it. Before me I saw a charismatic-looking young man. Even more attractive than his picture. He smiled.

"Hi," he said, raising his hand as he gave a slight wave.

"Come in," I said, smiling. Victor walked inside, reminding me of myself. He walked with his hands in his pockets and a smile on his face as he projected a feeling of nerves. It was a little cute. I walked him through the house to my room where Andrew, Renae and Candice were, rushing past mum and dad before they had a chance to ask questions or pry about how we knew each other.

"This is Victor, everyone," I introduced him, shutting the door behind us. Victor raised both his hands in the air, waving rapidly with his smile remaining.

"Hi people," said Victor. I grabbed his hand with excitement and guided him to sit down with me on the mattresses where we all sat and had formed a circle. We started to chat, and the conversation ran fluently. Online, Victor had been down-to-earth and informative, and in person he was grounded, funny and had an enticing personality. As my friends and he talked and laughed, I saw a guy I could picture my future with. His eyes were light blue and he had light brown hair, with his fringe swept to one side. His skin looked as though it could use a bit more sun, but I was hardly one to talk. After some time, Victor excused himself from the circle to use the toilet.

"So, what do you think?" I asked my friends under my breath as Victor left the room. They looked around in a positive manner.

"I think he's hilarious," said Andrew. I was shocked as I expected him to be the last one to speak.

"Yeah, he's really nice Michael," said Renae.

"He's a bit of a geek," said Candice.

"No, not at all. He's just out of touch with his school days and he's trying to act *cool*. I think it's cute," said Renae.

"Geek or not, that guy's funny!" said Andrew.

"I really like him," I said. "Like, really like him." It was so good to know I had the support of my friends, and being open and honest about it all was a relief. I had people to share my thoughts and emotions with.

The door to my bedroom opened. It was mum.

"Hi guys. Michael, I just thought I'd let you know your father and I are going to bed," she said.

"Thanks, mum," I replied. Mum gestured back to the bathroom with her hand held like a hitch hiker.

"Who's that?" she asked.

Renae jumped in to my rescue. "Oh that's a friend of mine from down south. I thought I'd invite him along," she lied. Mum smiled, saying it was nice of us to include him, and then left the room. Victor soon returned. The night continued, and it was a true night to savor, full of good memories. As the night drew on, we watched movies with a blanket between us all. Victor looked over at me and smiled while the colours of the movies projected onto his face in the dark, setting a calm and illuminant like comfort to the situation.

"I like you," he whispered.

"I like you too," I whispered back. He placed his hand on my leg and squeezed it, then released it and left it where it remained. He didn't rub, fondle or touch me elsewhere. He just held his hand on my leg and I leant my head on top of his shoulder, nestled up to him closely.

Once the movie finished, I asked if he would like to stay.

"I'd really like that," he whispered.

"Okay guys, let's take our mattresses to the lounge room," Candice instructed. "We don't want to intrude on snuggles!" Andrew laughed at her, he'd really lightened up, but then I supposed they were all staying. Even if a few rooms away.

"All right," Renae said, picking up the mattresses with Candice and Andrew as they marched on out. They shut the door behind them.

"Don't let the bed bugs bite... or Victor," called out Candice. I heard them giggling as they walked off. I looked over at Victor and he stood as he had when he'd first entered the house, with his hands in his pockets and a smile on his face. I walked up to him with confidence, knowing somewhat what I was doing, and placed my fingers in the two front pockets of his trousers, pulling him forward. I began to kiss him, but Victor pulled back and then rested his forehead on mine.

"Do you want to do this?" Victor asked, sweetly. His courtesy and nervousness turned me on, as if I had the power. As if I was the one in control.

"I do," I said, as I pulled him over to my bed with me by his trousers. I hopped onto the bed, dragging him on with me, then rolled him over so that I was on top. Reversing the position I had taken with Cameron, I wanted to be the one fucked this time. Leaning over the top of him, I started to undo the buttons of his shirt. He rubbed my legs and then began to undo my belt, ripping it off once undone. He unbuttoned and unzipped me, then reached inside my pants and underneath to grab my balls as he moved his fingers to caress them. I leant back in pleasure, before pulling off his unbuttoned shirt.

I undid his belt and trousers, then pulled them off too eager to take out his belt. Sitting back down on top of him, over his underwear, I nestled his firm cock between my arse cheeks. I felt its pulsating heat from underneath the cotton which kept our flesh from touching. I began to move forward and backward to tease him, and he pulled down my underwear, starting to wank me. The feeling of his hands' tight grip tugging my cock back and forth was irresistible. He spat at his hand and started to glide it over me. I leant over to my right and opened the chest of drawers beside my bed to grab a packet of condoms. Ripping the packet open, I moved his hand away, made my way down to his crotch to pull off his underwear, and as I did, I threw them to the side. Learning from Cameron, I placed the condom in my mouth and slipped it over Victor. As I pushed it down, he let out a moan of pure pleasure, while he entered my mouth as I rolled the condom down his cock. I knew he wanted this bad, and so did I. I was extremely aroused. Once the condom was on, I raised myself up to look at him, as I asked if he wanted to fuck me.

"Oh god yes, I'm dying to fuck you," he said. Raising my arse above him, I grabbed hold of his cock with one hand as I pulled one of my arse cheeks back with the other, and rubbed his tip around the surface of my anus to massage it. I shut my eyes and bit my lip, it felt fucking great.

"Go slow," I said, slowly moving down as he glided inside me. It really hurt at first. I mean, insanely painful. In shock, I pulled away.

"Ouch," I said.

"It's okay, Michael. We don't have to if you don't want to," said Victor.

"I want to," I said. I paused for a moment, resisting my bodies resistance.

"Take your time," said Victor, sweetly. I took a short breath, and then pushed myself back down onto him as he re-entered me, and it felt surprisingly good this time. The more I drew my body up and down, the better it felt. I moved up and down, while he slid in and out of me. It started to feel insanely amazing as my muscles loosened and my body gave in to the movement. He began to fuck me with his own strength as I held myself up with an arched back and my hands on the bed. It began to feel even more fantastic. As he fucked me, he wanked me off with his right hand, and I felt more incredible by the second. He fucked me and fucked me as he wanked me, and all of a sudden I burst with cum as he moaned and came inside me. I leant back down towards him and slowly pulled my waist forward while his dick slid out of me. I laid down beside him.

"That was freak-in unbelievable," I said.

"You're telling me," said Victor. He rolled towards me, and placed his arm on top of my chest as we drifted to sleep. I was on cloud nine.

9 FAGGOT

The last few months that led to graduation were truly brilliant. Victor asked me to be his boyfriend, officially, and Andrew and Renae got on well with him but, interestingly, Candice did not. Candice thought I could do better, and that I was too young to be in a relationship. Truth be told, I thought she was just looking forward to having a single *gay friend* when I came out. But now that I was spending most of my time with Victor, she wasn't as ecstatic as she initially reacted, in fact she felt a little distant. I never got to see Victor during the day as I still attended school, though he always texted me to see how my day was going and, to let me know that he was thinking of me. One lunch time at school I received a pleasant surprise when he actually visited me onsite in the schoolyard. As he approached, he pulled out a bunch of flowers from behind his back. I was so taken aback that I was speechless. Victor went in to kiss me, but I hesitated as I was surrounded by peers, peers other than my friends. If I leaned into that kiss it would be official; I would be *out*. Making an impulsive decision, I moved into the kiss and took the flowers. I felt people staring and glaring right away, and could hear gasps and sniggering comments from all directions.

A pair of students named Tom and Gus walked past at that very moment. The two weren't in any specialist course themselves, they were just a pair of local students. As they passed, Tom stopped and pulled Gus back in shock.

"What the fuck?" said Gus. Tom walked up to us as Gus followed.

"What's this, you're a fucking queer?" asked Tom. Andrew stood up and walked in front of them as I stood feeling helpless. Victor held my hand and stood beside me.

"No, he's not a fucking queer, dude. He's homosexual," said Andrew.

"Can you say homophobic?" Renae added.

"I'm not homophobic. I just don't appreciate two guys rubbing their disgusting life choices in my face!" shouted Tom. Victor let go of my hand and walked to stand beside Andrew.

"Come on, guys," Victor said. "I apologise. I didn't realise in this day and age students were still so backwards."

"Oh no, you didn't," called Gus as he took a swing at Victor. The hit sent Victor to the floor, and his nose bled on the pavement. Andrew went to have a go at Gus, but Tom held him back. I dropped to the floor by Victor's side.

"You'd be best to stay out of this, Drew! This beef is not with you," said Tom.

"Let it go Andrew," said Renae. "These fucktards will get what's coming to them. How about you think twice about making out with your girlfriend in the corner of the yard every lunch time before going around throwing fists at others, Gus?!" He walked over and moved his face up close to Renae.

"Because my girlfriend and I making our isn't foul," said Gus, pointing to Victor. He stood tall, straightened his collar and spat down at the floor towards Victor, and then walked off with Tom.

"Are you okay?" I asked Victor.

"Yeah, I'll be fine. But this was a stupid idea. I'm so sorry, Michael," he said.

"No, don't be stupid. This was the best thing anyone has ever done for me. I am so lucky. You are the sweetest," I said. I thought for a moment and, although the timing wasn't quite right, I just had to ask him.

"Will you be my date to the ball?"

"Are you kidding? Were you here just now?" said Victor.

"You're over-thinking it. The Ball will have teachers supervising, hotel staff and security. Let's give it to them. Push it in people's shitty faces. It's people like those two that have kept me from accepting who I am this whole time. Plus, it won't be the setting for them to do anything like this. They'd be stupid to leave an impression like that on everyone for the last event of school," I said.

"Maybe he's right," said Andrew.

"No, Andrew. If they can't handle a same-sex couple at the ball then they can leave," I said. "There's no one I'd rather spend that moment with than you, Victor. Why should I have to deprive myself of a student's most precious moment for people who aren't comfortable with me? That's their problem, not mine."

Victor eventually agreed. I agreed it was a risky move but if I wasn't going to make a stand, who would? If word spread about a same-sex couple at the ball, maybe others would feel one step closer to accepting who they were. Every little move counts, right? It was seeing Cameron be who he was that made me more comfortable in my own skin, in his confidence in his own. Whether I'd seen him again or not.

Victor left the school with a swollen nose, and I saw through my afternoon of classes. Andrew and I finished last class together and walked to the front, saying goodbye as we parted ways. I began to walk ahead down the stairway to get my bus, but was grabbed from behind in my tracks and dragged into some bushes. My heart jumped, and beat rapidly with fret. I looked around, this setting was familiar, cornered against a wall with bushes around me. Claustrophobia took hold of me. I was held down to the ground. My eyes focused and I saw Gus and Tom in front of me. They pulled their dicks out, taking turns at slapping me with them, as they knelt down to my level. I tried to scream but they shoved hands full of dirt in my mouth. Parts of the dirt was thrown into my eyes, and I couldn't see or breathe properly as I started to hyperventilate. I started inhaling the dirt. It felt like razors had made their way down my throat. I honestly thought I was going to die then and there.

"You like that, don't you faggot?" Gus said as he sat on my chest. "Oi, keep on the lookout, and don't watch you perv," Gus said to Tom. I couldn't see at this point, and virtually gave up trying to struggle, but the sound of slapping and panting suggested he was wanking himself on top of me. I felt spurts of semen hit my face as he groaned, it was the most degrading moment of my life, and I really did fear for my life.

"Hey, there's someone coming," said Tom. I heard him run from the scene.

"Fuck," murmured Gus as I heard his zipper. That was the last thing I remembered, before waking up in hospital.

"Hi, my little Angel," I heard mum's voice as I tried opening my eyes. It hurt for a moment, like sandpaper was against them. I slowly managed. I looked over to where there was a side table beside me, and caught sight that I was laying in a hospital bed. Mum and dad stood beside it. Mum was holding my hand. My eyes felt so dry. I looked over to find Andrew, Renae and Mr Stanley stood around the end of the bed. Mum stood up and leaned over to kiss me on the forehead, but she kept hold of my hand.

"Mum," I said.

"Yes, I'm here, sweetie. We're all here," said Mum. I saw Mr Stanley approach mum.

"I think it's best we leave Michael with his friends for a moment while we grab a coffee. We can come back later when the doctor is here." Mum nodded, and the two of them started to walk off. Dad stood and made eye contact with me, smiling a smile of empathy and care, before joining behind mum and Mr Stanley. Once they left, my friends gathered around me, close.

"Who did this to you?" asked Andrew.

"You know who," said Renae.

"You can't just assume that," said Andrew.

"No, she's right," I said, coughing. I used my arms to sit myself up and reached for some water beside me. Renae walked up and helped me pour it from the jug to the cup. I took the cup and sipped it. My throat felt sore and strained.

"So it was those bastards," said Andrew.

"Yeah, I don't know what happened exactly," I said.

"Well, they gave you a good kick in the head that's for sure," said Andrew.

"Those fuckers knocked me out to shut me up," I mumbled under my breath. "Unbelievable... Where's Victor?"

"Well, we haven't told him you're here. We thought you might not enjoy explaining his presence to your folks," said Renae.

"Yeah, that was probably best. Can you please not tell him? I'd prefer him not to know," I said. I didn't want him feeling worse than he already had for visiting me at school.

As the days passed, I ignored his calls, but just until my swelling went down. I was released from hospital, playing oblivious to the nurses and doctors on what had happened. There was no evidence of sexual abuse, so there were no tests and all the doctors had was a bruise on my head. It was Mr Stanley who had found me. He had pulled me out from the bush. As there was no mention of it, I suspect that as the dirt fell from my face, so did the semen, acting as a substance in-between it and my skin. I was furious to think that those boys were under the delusion that they could have done what they did because they disagreed with my choice of lifestyle. Hell, it was not even a choice, my mind developed this way on its own. I wasn't scared of them though. I was determined to seek revenge, and it boiled within me.

*

I went back to school the following week, with only a week of school remaining – then the Ball. Each time I passed Gus and Tom, I glared at them to let them know that I wasn't scared. If they tried anything again, I would be ready. Knowing that I had not told anyone what happened, I'm pretty sure they avoided trying anything again to provoke me or get caught. I called Victor to apologise with the excuse that my phone had been playing up. He spoke to me in tears, under the impression I had been angry at him for his surprise visit. I assured him that it was just some tech issues but that

I had needed to focus on the remainder of my studies at school too. He understood, despite the half truth.

*

The night of the ball arrived, and I only had the slightest mark remaining on my head. Andrew came over to my place and we got ready together. Finally dressed, Andrew and I stood in the bathroom looking at each other in our suits.

"Are you ready for this?" Andrew asked.

"Petrified," I answered. Not for the ball itself, but because I had decided this was the night that I would come out to my parents. If it turned sour, I planned to run off with Victor. If it didn't, I was hoping things would gradually move forward or at least stay the same. "Do you mind staying here while I talk with them?" I asked Andrew.

"No, not at all," he replied.

I walked out to the living room where my parents were sitting. They stood up and looked at me. Dad smiled and put his arm around mum, while Mum held her hands to her face as her eyes swelled with tears.

"Look at you. You're all grown up," she said. I looked at them both for a moment, almost ready to just let it pass. But I gathered myself and the courage, knowing that it had to be done.

"Mum, dad... can we sit down for a moment please?" I asked.

"Of course, sweetie, is everything all right?" Mum asked.

"Yes, everything's fine," I said, while we sat down. I held my hands together, and my right knee began to shake up and down with nervous energy. What passed as a few seconds felt like an hour, and I took a deep breath set to speak. "Mum."

"Yes?"

"Dad."

"Yes?"

"I love you both so much, and I've got something I've been meaning to tell you for some time now," I said.

"We love you too sweetie," said Mum, leaning over to grab my hands.

"You know I've been going through some stuff the last few years, and I'm sure you've both wondered what's been going on. Well, I'm here to tell you now. I'm asking for your acceptance. I am gay," I finished, freezing as I waited for a response. Mum let go of my hands and leant back to look at dad. He glanced at mum and then looked down at the floor. Mum began to cry.

"Ha," she said. "I don't know why I'm crying. I mean, I've known this for years. It's just hearing it is so... it's so real."

"You've known?" I asked.

"My little angel, of course I've known. I'm your mother. Call it mother's intuition," she said, wiping her tears away. "That's it then. Come here and give me a hug." She stood up and extended her arms to me. I stood and hugged her with my eyes clenched tight, consumed by happiness with her acceptance. I opened my eyes and looked down at dad who was still seated looking down at the floor.

"Dad," I said, sitting back down. Mum sat beside him and put her hand on his lap. "Tell me what you're thinking." Dad took an even deeper breath than I had and released the air out from his lungs as his cheeks blew up and deflated like a blow fish.

"Well, son. I suppose there's heterosexual, there's bisexual and then there's homosexual. And if you've, ah, come to terms with being homosexual, then I guess that's all there is to it." I stood to hug him, as he moved away awkwardly. "I just need a bit of space for a moment, son. It's nothing personal. I just need some space."

"Yeah, sure, whatever you need," I said, happy that he had not pushed me through a window. "There is one more thing."

"And what's that, sweetie?" Mum asked.

"My date. Do you remember Renae's friend from down south?"

"Vaguely," Mum said.

"It wasn't a friend of hers from down south. Victor is actually my boyfriend, and he's taking me to the ball tonight," I explained.

Mum walked up to me and grabbed my hands. "Let's hope he brings you a corsage then," she said as she kissed me on the cheek.

"I think I need to sit down again," dad said, as he sat back on the couch.

"Oh, just let your father be. He'll be all right, we've always suspected this."

"Okay, if you say so." The doorbell rang. My heart pounced.

"How about I answer it this time? I'll give him a nice warm welcome to our home. You sit down," mum said as she smiled and winked.

"I'll just be in my office," dad said as he stood and walked away. I sat down with my back turned away from the front door. I heard it open, and then Victor's voice, as mum welcomed him.

"I'm Marie, Michael's mum. It's a true pleasure to meet you," she said. I heard them walking over together. "Michael, Victor's here." I stood and turned around. He wore a suit, fitted to his body like a model, with a box in his hand.

"Hi," I said. "You look amazing."

"Well, so do you," said Victor. "May I?" he asked mum, gesturing to walk over to me.

"Of course," she said. Victor approached and kissed me. I closed my eyes and licked my lips as he pulled away slowly, opening my eyes again. *FLASH*, mum had taken a photo.

"Get together then," she said.

"Hey, how about me?" said Andrew, as he joined us. The next few moments were some precious memories. Smiles, friends, family and a whole lot of sentiment. Victor opened up the box he held in his hand, and inside was the most exquisite corsage which he pinned onto my jacket.

"This way, no one can call you a girl, your sexuality doesn't make you any less of a man," said Victor, referring to the tradition of placing it on the wrist. "Hey, what's this?" He said, as he held his hand against the bruise on my face.

"Oh, nothing," I said.

"Some idiots punched him out. Didn't even take his wallet or phone, isn't that the strangest thing?" said Mum. Victor looked at me, not convinced.

"It's okay, babe," I said to him. "Now I've got to put some product in my hair."

I walked to the bathroom and combed my hair back, I could hear Andrew, Victor and mum laughing, and it put a real heartfelt smile on my face. Spraying my hair in place, my dad walked into the bathroom.

"Listen, mate. I'm a little squeamish right now, but I'll be okay. Don't think I disapprove or I'm against it or anything," he said.

"Thanks, dad," I said. He walked up to me and put his arm around me.

"You're my son. You're the same boy you've always been. Nothing changes that. I know Luke and I play a bit of rough and tough, but when I'm with any mates of mine or at work, I want you to know you're the one I speak of most proudly. You're so young, and you've made some real accomplishments. Be proud. I love you son," said dad, patting his hand on my shoulder. "Now go take over that dance floor, son."

I walked back out to where Victor, Andrew and mum were, as dad followed behind me. From the front of the house, a horn honked.

"That'll be the Jeep," said Andrew. We all moved towards the front door, and mum opened it for us as Victor and Andrew walked out. As I approached I hugged and kissed both mum and dad on my way out.

"Have a great time, you hear? And please be careful," said mum. I told her I would and began to walk off. "Michael! That's a good-looking young man you've got there." I smiled and thanked her. Walking ahead, we saw Renae in the car with her boyfriend in the driver's seat. Renae stood up in the Jeep and waved.

"Hey boys, ready to see out high school!?" she shouted.

"Ready as ever," shouted Andrew, as he ran and jumped into the Jeep. Victor walked me over, arms linked, and helped me to step up into it. Mum and dad walked behind us and wished us all farewell.

"You all look out for each other now, you hear," said dad. "Especially these two. I want my son back home in one piece." He smiled and winked at me.

10 LAST DAYS AT LUMIERE

Driving to the School Ball, I looked around at Andrew, Renae and her boyfriends in the vehicle, laughing and interacting with each other. Silently taking in the moment. I remembered back to the night I had walked home from my primary school dance and saw the group of teenagers walking along together on the street. Wishing for a friend. Now, I had two, at least. As Renae's boyfriend drove us towards the hotel hosting our ball, the entrance of the building shone bright in the distance, draped with white twinkling fairy lights. We pulled in to the queue for the entrance, where Limos and Hummers were lined up in front of us. Valets and bell boys helped students out of vehicles as they welcomed them. While we waited, there was a sense of excitement and sentiment that I felt was within each of us. It felt infectious.

"Here we are folks, it's finally here, the god-damn ball," said Andrew.

"I know, can you believe it?" said Renae.

"Where's Candice tonight?" I asked.

"She said she already had a ride," answered Renae.

We pulled up to the entrance and got out of the Jeep. Renae's boyfriend threw the keys to the Valet. The five of us walked towards the entrance and Victor linked his arm in mine. From behind us, someone called out our names.

"Yoo-hoo!" shouted Candice. We looked behind us, and there on her arm was Gus, as her date. "What are you doing, guys?"

"Ha-ha, hey faggot, put it here," said Gus, placing his hand in the air for a high five. They were both clearly intoxicated. We all looked at them in disgust. The word, infuriated me. But I wasn't about to let him ruin the start of my night. "No high five then. Man, that cuts deep," said Gus. Tom came up behind Gus and pushed him viciously.

"Move along, man," said Tom.

"What are you doing, bud?" asked Gus.

"I said move along," repeated Tom. Gus looked blankly and then drunkenly laughed, stumbling back on to Candice's arm as they walked inside. Tom walked up to me.

"Listen, I'm sorry about what happened. It never meant to go that far. Gus got carried away, and I'm really ashamed of what he did," he said.

"It was both of you. I'm not interested in your excuses," I said, glaring at Tom.

"I didn't..."

"Hey, he said he's not interested," said Andrew, coming in between us both.

"I'm just trying to make amends," said Tom, backing away.

"Make it somewhere else," said Andrew. Tom turned and walked inside ahead of us.

"Who was that guy? Is he the one that did this to you?" asked Victor, pointing to my bruise.

"You know what? It wasn't even anything. Just a bump against a wall, that's all," I said, trying to keep Victor calm. He looked displeased.

"I'll look after you tonight," he said, kissing me on the head. We gathered together and walked in through the front doors into the foyer. The decor was divine; the ceilings hung with crystal chandeliers and the carpet which lined the floor was a deep red. We followed signage which pointed to the ballroom where our event was being held, Victor still linked to my arm.

As we got to the ballroom door, we stood to the back of a line waiting to get in. Mr Stanley stood with a file and pen marking off names as they arrived. As we reached the front, our eyes made contact. He looked down at my arm linked with Victor's, then back up at me and smiled.

"I'm glad to see you here," he said.

"Thank you, sir, and thank you for helping me," I said.

"Don't mention it. Just do me a favour. If you do remember what happened, do tell me," he said with concern. I smiled and nodded, keeping my memory to myself. "Don't let me keep you then, get inside and dance it up," he said. We walked inside. The atmosphere was unbelievable, the music was pumping and lights beamed onto the walls and flooring.

As the night progressed, we said hi to teachers who had taught us through the years and ate a three course meal fit for royalty. Andrew, Renae, her boyfriend and I started dancing on the dance floor, and were having the time of our lives. Victor remained seated at the table, insisting he could not dance. The dance floor was packed and we moved, full of energy. Everyone united. Everything that had bothered me, made me anxious or depressed me in the past drifted from my mind. It was a celebration. A joyous occasion. Another chapter of my life coming to a close, this time on a more positive note. With magnificent people by my side, my bestest buddy in the world, Andrew, most of all.

"If you could each take your seats, we will be making the announcement of this year's King and Queen shortly," announced Ms Martinovich over the microphone, standing centre stage. The people on the dance floor began to part, and we with them, took our seats. I looked around for Victor, as when we'd returned to our table he wasn't at his seat.

"You haven't seen Victor, have you?" I asked the table.

"Sorry, dude," said Andrew. Renae shook her head with a frown, snuggled up to her boyfriend beside her. I sat, puzzled, and then looked towards the stage as Ms Martinovich began to speak.

"I'm glad to see such a large attendance here tonight. It seems like yesterday I welcomed you all. I won't bore you with any formalities as I'm sure you're all dying to find out who won your votes for this year's King and Queen," she said. A teacher walked up to Ms Martinovich on the stage with two envelopes, passing them to her. Opening the first, she brought the microphone back to her mouth. "Boys and girls, it is my pleasure to announce that this year's King of Lumiere College of the Arts is... Simon Abercrombie," she announced.

I looked over to Simon's table, where he expressed excitement and surprise. It was a swell feeling seeing someone surprised like that. Although we hadn't stayed friends, he was certainly the first impression I had at Lumier, and my future possible peers. He'd never been nasty to me, we had simply drifted to different social circles, still with a smile to acknowledge one another from time to time. I was happy that such a sport won. Simon rose up from his table and walked across the dance floor to the stage. Mr Culver crowned him, and Mrs Cornel stood waiting with the crown for Queen.

Simon accepted a loud applause, and took a bow. Then Ms Martinovich continued to speak.

"And so, the moment all you girls have been waiting for. The Queen of this year is..." Everyone in the room kept silent. I looked around to see many faces in hope, stress and full of nerves. Looking back up at the stage, I imagined accepting the award myself - whether it was as king or queen-queer! I didn't have anything against Simon, but I did envy the popularity a little, and the applause of accomplishment which he received this night. An applause received simply for being himself. "...Natalie Baker!" Ms Martinovich finished the announcement.

Natalie – who had also been in the Musical Theatre course - walked and accepted her crown as the crystals covering it shimmered in the lights. Her face filled with gratitude and delight. I could only imagine the feelings she was experiencing and hoped that one day I'd feel the adoration, cherishment and idolisation which she received that night, accepting her crown. I marvelled her. After receiving her crown, Simon escorted her arm in arm off the stage, as they both shared smiles and blew kisses to us all. Both teachers and peers approached to congratulate and praise them. All of a sudden, I began to feel a touch of callousness.

"On that note. I need to use the bathroom," I said, excusing myself from the table. The admiration in the room being a little too much for me. If only I knew back then how that admiration didn't always mean, good. How it attracted other admired. How the admired, were not always well meaning. How the admired, could be corrupt.

I stood and walked to the bathroom door in my own world, imagining being a person who was admired and loved by many – a crown on my head. I walked into the bathroom, heading straight for the first cubical on my left, and as I pushed open the cubicle door I found Tom turn to look back at me with surprise. His trousers and underwear were around his ankles and his bum cheeks exposed, he'd been thrusting back and forth into a guy bent over the toilet bowl. The guy turned around, as Tom gasped, and it was Victor. Victor, was bent over the toilet bowl. It was Victor, Tom was fucking. Victor, caught in a despicable act, morphed a face of deep shock and regret. As soon as his eyes registered that I had opened the door onto him and Tom, he stood up fast with a look of panic in his eyes.

"Michael, Michael, babe," he began to speak, reaching out for me.

"Save it!" I shouted. My stomach turned, I was absolutely disgusted. I quickly realised I'd much rather be back out in a room of smiles and admiration. In a room with my friends. In a room with my bestest buddy in the world. In a room with people who had proven themselves loyal to me. I didn't let Gus's disgusting derogatory term ruin this night and I wasn't about to let Victor. I had my whole life ahead of me now, I didn't need him. I wasn't upset nor distraught, but rather found myself pity the two guys in front of me. Having just had one of the best times of my life, I wasn't going to let anything or anyone get me down. Not this night. The fucker wasn't worth it. My face blanked over and my care factor was zero.

Tom and Victor began to pull up their pants in a hurry.

"Fuck, Michael. It could have been you but you weren't interested," said Tom.

"What the fuck?"

"I tried to talk to you" he tried to explain. I rolled my eyes in continued disgust.

"You're right. I'm into men with more balls than you," I said, a little confused and unable to comprehend what I had just seen and heard. "Faggots." I walked off back to my table, leaving them to finish each other off.

"So, I just found Tom fucking Victor in the cubicle," I said. The whole table's eyes widened in astonishment.

"What!? That dickhead," said Andrew.

"Andrew, I honestly couldn't give a flying fuck. I'm here with you guys, my best and most amazing friends in the whole wide world. I'm out to my parents who have accepted me for who I am, and I've got my whole life ahead of me," I said, reassuring both him and myself that I was not to be pitied. Victor and Tom came running up to the table.

"Michael, let me explain. When I suspected it was Tom that did this to you I went looking for him, and then…" said Victor, before I cut him off.

"We know each other's names now, do we?" I asked.

"This stays between us, right, Michael?" interrupted Tom.

"Oh yes, Tom. I haven't slipped up yet with any of our secrets, have I?" I said. Tom looked as if a guilty man standing in court, with nothing to say. "The pair of you should get lost before I decide to announce you as Queen B1 and Queen B2 over the microphone," I said, as I grabbed my drink and stood up. "You guys want to dance and keep this party going?" I asked Andrew, Renae and her boyfriend. They agreed, also standing, and we left Tom and Victor behind. They deserved each other.

The rest of the night was seriously magnificent, and we danced for hours. As we danced, I looked around the room at the coloured lights on the ceiling and the smiles on my friends' faces. I closed my eyes to take in the music as it played, and as the night came to an end, I finally experienced that saying that *all good things coming to an end*. I was looking forward to the next good thing. We walked out from the hotel to where the valet had our jeep running for us. Ahead of us, Candice and Gus stumbled out on to the road. They were laughing and giggling as cars honked their horns and swerved around them.

"Far out," said Andrew. I watched as their pathetic selves shouted at oncoming traffic and Candice trying to drag Gus back off the road, laughing as she did so. Candice ran back on to the grass out front of the hotel and called for Gus to come join her, barely able to hold herself up leaning on her bent knees for support. Her dress was pretty worse for wear.

"Dickhead," said Renae's boyfriend, as he jumped into the drivers seat. He started to pull out once we all got in and I looked over to Andrew and smiled. I decided to tell Gus exactly what I thought of him. I stood up in the Jeep and shouted out.

"Hey Gus… Fuck you!"

Gus turned around, and a huge screeching noise saturated the night. Within half a second of Gus catching my eyes, a car crashed into him. Candice screamed and ran up to his body as traffic started to break and come to a grinding halt, congesting the road.

"Fuck, man," said Andrew. Renae covered her face and screamed.

"Oh my god," she said. People began running over to help — not that they could. Everyone in the car looked at each other in a state of shock. When they looked ahead to the accident, the night stood silent for a moment, as Candice's screams echoed into the distance. I smirked to myself. I felt what some may call deranged, but I called it satisfaction. If only Victor and Tom could have joined him.

Once the traffic started to die down, Renae's boyfriend drove off. Passing the scene, an ambulance and police vehicles had arrived with their lights flashing, lighting up the darkened sky. Andrew stared, still in shock, and Renae turned away with tears streaming down her face as her boyfriend rubbed her leg with one hand and steered with the other. I, however, looked dead on at his mangled head and beat-up body on the road. I imagined driving the car that hit Gus myself, pushing my foot down hard on the accelerator with his drunken body ahead. *SPLAT*, all over the windscreen, his body would have rolled up and over the top of the car and into the air, hitting the ground head first as it cracked open on impact. I further imagined getting out of my car and walking up to the body, with bits of his brain splattered over the road. Kneeling down, I'd scoop his brains with my index finger and taste the flavour of justice.

*

My mind began to fuzz, coming back to reality as Renae repeated my name and shook me softly. The car ride home had been a blur. As we pulled up to my parents' driveway, Renae asked if I was okay as she sniffed, not even okay herself.

"I'm fine," I said.

"They offered me a lift home, buddy. Will you be all right tonight?" asked Andrew.

"I'll be fine," I answered. Renae leaned over from the front seat to hug me and grasped me tight as she said goodbye. Andrew patted me on the back and then held his hand in place for a few seconds longer.

"Call me if you need anything," said Andrew.

"I will," I promised, hopping out of the jeep. I began to walk up the drive, then turned around and waved as they drove off. They had treated me as if I was upset by the incident, as if Gus had been a close family member, but in fact I was in rather high spirits, and I did not feel even an ounce of remorse for it. This chapter of my life, to my mind, could not have ended more perfect.

*

We held one more event at hand, graduation, arriving instantaneously. Sat in the old school hall, we wore satin robes in front of a stage which was set for presentations. I looked around me, much like I did the first day of Musical Theatre class. Not looking at people to see if I'd befriend or take a fancy to them, but looking at people who I'd shared five years of my life with. To the corner of my eye, I saw Tom walking across to his seat, looking like a ghost as his friends comforted him. I looked back behind me spotting mum, dad and Luke in the not too far distance. I waved at them, and they waved back. Mum waved most enthusiastically with a large and proud smile on her face. I turned back around, sat in between Renae and Andrew. I looked at each of them separately, placing one arm around Andrew and my other on Renae's lap. I knew the three of us were destined to be friends for life.

Once the ceremony started, the principal spoke words of advice, consideration and admiration directed to us all. He then handed the microphone to Ms Martinovich who took a subtle but deep breath, and held silence for a brief few seconds. Looking up to the students before her, she began to speak.

"Today you each leave behind a time of your life which took great strides in molding you, and has taken part in who you've become today, and who you will be in the future. However, we also leave behind the memory of a student who will not get to move on past this stage of his life, as he left us in death on the night of the school ball last weekend..." As she continued to speak, I kept looking around me. These people were blinded, not seeing the monster that Gus was, or what a favour that driver did for the world that night. I started to imagine what would have happened if I got up and walked down the aisle to the microphone to educate the students, parents and teachers about who Gus really was. Would more students that were attacked by him come out and take a stand? I surely could not have been the first. My mind started to fuzz.

*

The next thing I recall is waking up back in hospital. Mum and dad sat by my side, with Andrew and Renae standing at the end of my bed, again. A doctor approached. The doctor leant down and pulled the lids of my eyes up while he shone a torch into my pupils.

"How are you feeling, young man?" the doctor asked.

"I'm all right. What happened?" I asked, looking over at mum and dad.

"You blacked out, sweetheart. Right between Andrew and Renae," said mum.

"Did I graduate?" I asked. Mum laughed and nudged her chair forward, starting to stroke my head.

"Yes, you graduated, my little angel" she said. The doctor placed a scan against a light box on the wall. It showed what looked like an eagle's eye view of the inside of my head. The scan showed the squiggly shape of a brain, and in parts some rather dark matter. The doctor started to talk, and pointed to the dark matter in the scan.

"There's no easy way to say this, but this is what we call a plague of the brain. It appears as though there has been a build-up in clusters of protein fragments. There seems to be a few clusters which have been dormant for some time, but other areas are active, brought on after that nasty impact to your head" he explained. "I'm sorry to say this Michael, but there is active existing matter building between your brain's nerve cells."

"This is all great, doctor, but give it to us straight and cut the bullshit," said dad. The doctor stepped away from the scan. He sat down on the bed next to me and looked at mum and dad.

"Basically the tissue in your son's brain is reducing in nerve cells quicker than that the average healthy brain in a boy his age. Depending on how quickly the clusters tangle – that is, if they do – we may see early signs of onset Alzheimer's. Not that that is what this is, but this certain disease does show the same symptoms in the brain," he explained. "And I'm legally obliged to advise you that, in some cases," he paused and looked at me, "it can lead to death." The room filled with a stillness that I can only describe as a sense of lull. I couldn't hear one breath from anyone in that room. The word death didn't frighten me as you'd have thought it might. But the reaction and emotions of others frightened me significantly. The thought of leaving all of these beautiful people behind. That, frightened me.

"Is there anything we can do? Treatment?" asked dad, as my friends looked at me in pity, and mum clenched my hand.

"Stress is a major halter. Reduce stress from his life in any way possible," the doctor said. "But there is no treatment as such for this, I'm afraid." He didn't look at me again, not even a glance, just talked to my parents as if I was one of the four walls in the room. My mind began to drift, and again it started to fuzz. "It's a rare disease, and much like bleeding gums can come back and go away at various times dependent on pressure..." he continued to speak, and my mind fuzzed out as I saw mum burst into tears.

11 THE SCENE

Officially graduated from high school, and not under any pressure to find work or study due to my newly diagnosed condition, I led a life which for a while I could not fault. Meeting Andrew and Renae out in the city for lunch and, shopping, became a large part of my life. My parents had given me an allowance so that I didn't need to stress about money or finances. One night Renae invited Andrew and I out to her cousin's party. Her gay cousin in fact, which at the time she forgot to mention. It was endearing actually, that he wasn't a *token gay cousin* to her. When Andrew and I arrived outside the address Renae had forwarded on to us, we pulled up on the street and saw two guys making out in the back seat of a parked car on the street.

"Hop in there," Andrew said, jokingly. I hit him on the shoulder.

"I'm not a swinger," I said, laughing. We hopped out of the car and walked to the front door. The house was an immaculate double storey with a large water fountain feature and front windows which reached from the first floor to the second. As we stood in front of the door, we heard squealing and loud music coming from inside the residence.

"Pumping party. Should we bother with the doorbell?" Andrew questioned.

"Nah," I said, opening the door as I laughed. As I pushed the door open, we entered a house full of the most diverse pairs and groups of people I had ever seen in one place at one time. Ever, actually. Straight in front of us was a staircase which spiraled up to the second floor, and sitting on it was gay couple making out, or I might say *dry humping* one another, lipstick lesbians drinking beer and talking smack, and a few butch in the mix. Plastics with low cut tops seemed to run about the house with cups of punch, while other more civilized individuals gathered in the kitchen in intellectual conversation.

"This is freakin' awesome," Andrew said, grabbing the front of my shirt as he dragged me through the house. We walked through, taking each step on beautiful marble flooring, and found our way to the back yard, which seemed to be the heart of the party complete with a multi-coloured lit-up pool. As we stepped outside, Renae spotted us from afar and ran over with a drink in her hand.

"Boys, you made it!" she screamed and hugged us, spilling her drink as she talked without noticing.

"I've never seen you like this," I said.

"Like what?" she asked.

"Completely fucking written off!" Andrew added. Renae looked at him blankly and then back at me.

"I'm so, so glad you came. You know you mean the world to me, don't you? Don't you?" she said, repeating herself.

"What's with all the pride party?" I asked.

"Well, since school finished, mum said it would be good to get to know the cousins, and what do you know? My cousin, Rob, is gay. Gay, gay, gay!" she said, repeating herself. An incredibly good-looking tanned guy with blonde hair and grey-green eyes walked up to us and wrapped one of his arms around Renae.

"Who are these two good looking young lads?" he asked.

"This is Andrew, and this is Andrew. And this is Michael. He's the one that is gay too," said Renae. The good-looking guy laughed.

"I think it's nearly bed time for you, Renae," he said.

Renae grabbed his hand and took it off of her, then stood tall.

"No Rob, no bed. Shots! Shots! Shots! Shots!" Renae shouted, revealing that the good-looking guy was her cousin, and she marched off to the pool bar area. Yes, a pool bar area. Rob laughed and watched her march off then looked back at us.

"Wait for me," called Andrew, as he followed not far behind her. Rob smiled and looked at me.

"So, you're Michael," he said. "Renae has told me a bit about you."

"That's funny, as she's told me nothing about you," I said. Rob laughed.

"Yeah, well until now it's just been Christmas dinners with the aunts, uncles and grandparents. But little Renae's now all grown up. Say, can I get you a drink?" he offered.

"Sure."

"Come on," he said as he held my hand, leading me over to the bar. He wore bright yellow shorts, with a bright blue and green Hawaiian shirt worn loosely and unbuttoned. His hands were soft, and his scent was alluring. At the bar, he ordered me a strawberry daiquiri.

"You have your own bartender," I said, astonishingly.

"Nah, it's self serve. Loui just likes working the bar and showing off his muscles. What about you? What do you like to do?" asked Rob, in a sensual manner.

"I like you," I blurted out, without thinking. Rob laughed, as Loui gave us our drinks.

"That's very flattering," he said.

"I meant to say…"

"I know, I know," he interrupted. "You like me. It's okay – I'm a likeable guy. Come sit with me." Rob led me over to a bench beside the pool, and he sat down. I sat down on the opposite end of the bench so there was some space between us. Rob rubbed the surface of the gap between us, gesturing for me to sit closer. I smiled, bashfully, then slid closer. "You coming to the club later?" Rob asked.

"I'm underage," I said.

"I'll get you in," said Rob. I smiled, raising my drink to my lips to take a sip. Rob and I talked for what seemed like a lifetime, as he charmed me with a hypnotic stare with those grey-green eyes and, a smooth and confident and all at the same time seductive voice. After a while, Renae and Andrew joined us at the table, and for the whole night we talked while the party hit its peak, until it came to an end. The night had been full of many drinks, much flirtation and a lot of laughter.

"Looks like the party is moving on. Shall I call a cab?" asked Rob. Within half an hour, a cab pulled up and the four of us got inside. Andrew sat in the front, and Rob and I sat in the back next to Renae who passed out against the cab's window. Andrew started speaking drunkenly with the driver and, with Renae asleep beside us, Rob undid my trousers and stuck his hand inside beginning to massage me, going from an unexpected flaccid state to instantaneously stiff. He moved up closer to me and bit my earlobe.

"We're going to have fun tonight," Rob whispered. I was absolutely infatuated with the guy. He then withdrew his hand and redid my trousers. The cab pulled up outside a club which had a full line of people outside waiting to get in.

"Renae's passed out" said Andrew. "Maybe we should take her home." Rob grabbed my hand and mouthed at me to stay with him. *Don't go.*

"I think I'll head out with Rob. Can you look after her?" I asked, my body intoxicated with raging hormones.

"Dude, are you serious?" said Andrew.

"Fine by me," said Rob, as he leant over me to open the car door and mouthed at me to *get out*.

"Yeah, sorry Andrew," I said as I got out of the car. A moment like this was too exciting to pass up, and I knew Renae would be okay in Andrew's care. "I'll make it up to you!" Rob got out and pulled me away from the cab. I looked back at Andrew and could see the disappointment in his eyes through the cab window, before turning around to the sounds of a DJ mix. Rob bypassed the line and greeted security with a nod. They let us straight through, not even asking for ID.

"Told ya," said Rob. I laughed. Without even taking in the transition, we had ventured our way into the most indescribable place. There were gay men dancing, gay men making out, gay men drinking, gay men at the bar and gay men serving from the bar. "Welcome to *Para-dice'etcya*," said Rob. The club was pumping. He guided us through a crowd of hot, sweaty men and, as we made our way to the centre of the dance floor, he stopped and turned around, pulling me in so our bodies touched as we danced.

Rob thrust himself upon me and turned his face in to kiss me. We started making out while the club lights shone over us and the music pumped out around us. It was an incredible night, at the time it felt as though it surpassed the ball. I didn't know Rob, but he made me feel good that night. Alive. We danced for a while longer, and then he shouted over the music into my ear.

"Come with me, babe," he said, grabbing my hand as we made our way away from the dance floor. "I want you to meet some people." He dragged me away and introduced me to a group of large characters. They felt my chest, rustled my hair, pinched my cheeks and groped my butt.

"He's a cutie," one of them said.

"Fresh scene meat," shouted another.

"Oh girl, he's so fresh he needs to mature a little before we consider tasting him," one laughed. They all joked while they drank, smoked, and some chewed gum. Some of them wore singlets so loose you could see their nipples, and others wore shirts so tight you could see the definition of their bodies in the material. The guys all had their own taste in dress, that's for sure. One wore a cap off to the side, another wore a barrette, and one guy was completely shirtless, in tight jeans and a pair of heels.

"Absolute!" Rob called out. There she fucking was. I remember looking ahead to the back of a tall and slender female figure, with long straight sleek lime-green strands of hair which fell perfectly to mid-waist. She turned around, her hair whipping around with her, before falling perfectly back into place. In front of me stood someone at least six foot tall,

174

with not only lime-green hair, but dark-green glitter lips and arched eyebrows which sparkled and glistened in the club lights. Her eyes were defined by lines of colour, with long lashes both on the top and bottom of their eyelids. Their skin was contoured to perfection, and covered with gorgeous tones of foundation as if photoshopped on a computer. "Michael, meet her grandness, Angelica Absolute," introduced Rob. Absolute walked up to me in her vibrant outfit, speckled with glitter dust and chiffon which blew in the light breeze.

"Hi doll," she said. I was stunned for words.

"H-hi," I stuttered.

"Ain't never seen a drag queen before, huh doll?" she asked.

"No, sorry. Excuse my ignorance. You're gorgeous."

"Oh sweetie. You're fresh meat – you can be as ignorant as you want. Just wait until you're a queen and then you'll be in trouble." We both laughed. The rest of the night was unreal. Rob had brought me into a brand new world, where I didn't feel self conscious about how I acted, talked or held myself. I felt free to be myself. My campery heightened with the campness around me. I talked, danced and partied all night long. I never knew people could enjoy themselves so much. If only I knew what Paradice'etcya would become for me.

*

The next morning, I woke up in bed in a strange room with Rob by my side. Rob rolled over and placed his arm around me.

"Good morning, mister," he said.

"Good morning. What happened?" I asked.

"What happened is we had a fucking fantastic night, that's what," he said.

"So I didn't pass out or anything" I asked, worried about another graduation episode.

"No, no. You just had the time of your life and then clung on to me so tight I had to bring you to bed with me. It was kind of sweet, actually," he said. I sighed in relief – it was just a drunken moment of missing memories. Not the fuzz which I had been experiencing lately.

"So, we didn't...?" I asked, implying sex.

"No, we didn't," said Rob, assuring me that we had done nothing. "I know, such a shame." He nudged me as he laughed. I liked Rob. He was sweet, funny and charming, but in a cheeky way. "So, how'd you enjoy what you remember of your first night on the scene then?"

"The scene?" I asked.

"Yeah, that's what we call it."

"Well, I met you, which was nice, but the dancing was pretty good too," I said.

"And Absolute?"

"The drag queen? I couldn't take my eyes off of her."

Rob kicked off the covers and got up out of bed with a smile on his face. That morning he cooked me a scrumptious omelette, and made me a delicious coffee with whipped cream on top. He certainly was living the life. After enjoying breakfast, Rob collected my dish and took it out to the kitchen. I followed behind him and stood by the kitchen bench. After rinsing the dishes, he left them in the sink and came up to me, with both of us in only our underwear.

"Let's get rid of these," he said, tugging at the elastic which held my mine up. At the slightest suggestion, I was firm. We spent the rest of the morning back in his bed, indulging in foreplay and multiple orgasms. I had never cum so damn much. That afternoon I laid on his bed, looking at him while he lay fast asleep. I looked at his beautifully tanned skin, wonderfully formed hair, and at his incredibly toned body. Although it had been only one night and a day, at the time, I fell completely and utterly head over heels for the guy. Looking back, it was nothing more than hunger and lust.

The weeks that followed were spent dreaming about Rob when I was apart from him, and day-dreaming about what I wanted to do to him when I was with him. He took me out, not only to the club, but also on dates to cafes and restaurants for dinner. Although I'd enjoyed my time with Rob, and it became more and more apparently clear that he enjoyed his time with me, I was always a little wary because of my encounter with Victor. Rob was regularly on his phone, claiming to be for work. One particular night we were out at the club, and he was on his phone throughout what seemed like the entirety of the evening. I kept my eye glued to him with curiosity while trying to keep conversation going with those around me. Inside at the bar with a few of his friends, Rob leant over after putting his phone away and said he had to go to the bathroom. Left with his friends, I twiddled my fingers for a moment and then, driven by anxiety, excused myself and set off to look for Rob. Walking through the dance floor, people persisted to look me up and down while grabbing my groin and crotch as I passed. Being a regular occurrence on the dance floor I turned a blind eye to it, fobbing off the clubbers as I continued to look for Rob. When I made it to the bathroom I walked ahead to the start of the line, asking after him. People shook their heads, uninterested. I made my way back out into the loud, pumping music and searched around the club over and over again. I could not find him, but I did bump into Absolute.

"Angelica," I said. She turned around, this time in a fluorescent purple outfit and wig.

"Baby doll, how's things? Still fresh?" she asked.

"As fresh as I can be. You haven't seen Rob have you?"

"No sorry, doll. Sometimes he heads over to our office to say hi to management. Do you want to come with me and we'll take a look?" she asked. I nodded. She took my hand and walked me to a door which said *Staff Only*. As she opened the door, ahead of us was a short hallway with two bears in leathered straps fucking up against the wall.

"Get out of here, Jimmy," said Absolute as we walked past them.

"Two more seconds," Jimmy puffed.

"Out!" she shouted, looking back at them and pointing to the door through which we just entered. Absolute turned back around to me and apologised, then unlocked the next door. We entered and she shut the door behind us. We walked into a room which had a couple of wooden desks and a few stacks of paper by a couple of computers.

"Hmm, not here," said Absolute, putting the key into her bra.

"Does he have a key to this room?" I asked. Absolute looked blank for a moment, then laughed.

"Oh, how silly of me. I'm the only management on sight tonight. Whoops!" She walked past me to a desk and began to rummage through the drawers. "Now, there's a sneaky bottle of vodka in here somewhere if you'd like a shot. You keen, doll?"

"No, I'm okay. I'm just rather keen to find Rob," I said.

"Baby doll," she said, and stopped looking for the vodka. She walked up to me. "You know Rob isn't the most faithful boy, don't you? He's not one to tie himself down for long."

"Rob and I have a connection," I protested. Absolute gave me a look as if to say *you poor thing*, and she held my face with both her hands.

"They alllll have a connection with Rob," she said. She started to glide her hand down my chest and leaned into my body. I could feel her warm breath on my neck. I froze instantly, thinking perhaps she had lured me here for something else. I clenching my eyes shut, just like back in first grade, hoping it wouldn't go on. Her hand stopped at my waist.

"So young. So fresh. I could do things to you that you couldn't even begin to imagine, young Michael."

"I'd rather you didn't, Angelica," I said, speaking up.

"Oh sweet baby doll. Open your eyes. It's okay," she said. I slowly opened them and looked at her.

"You might not want it now, but you come back to me when you do," she said, and then wandered over to the office door and opened it as she gestured my exit.

"Welcome to the scene," she said as I walked away.

Walking back out into the club, I made my way to the exit and bumped into Rob.

"Where have you been?!" I shouted over the music.

"Sorry, babe. The bathroom queue was huge," he said, grabbing my waist to embrace me. I brushed his hands away. He felt sweaty.

"I looked for you there," I said.

"Well, that's where I was," he replied. I shook my head in disappointment and walked off past the crowd of drunk clubbers. Rob came after me and grabbed my arm to turn me back to him. I bent down and grabbed my head, I was in pain.

"Babe, are you okay?"

"No. Can we just go back to yours?" I asked.

"Okay babe, let's go," he said.

If only I hadn't met Rob. If only he hadn't dragged me to that place. If only I'd gone back with Andrew and Renae. Maybe none of this would have ever happened. Maybe I wouldn't be looking at myself in the mirror drained of everything. Drained of life. Maybe I wouldn't be preparing to hack at Absolute's chest with a knife. But then, maybe it all needed to happen. Maybe it's all meant to be. Maybe I'm the one that will set things right. The bitch, and her little minions, have it coming. I've got to do this. I can't let this horrifying crap go on any longer. Who knew what else they had done. What else they had covered up. I've just got to walk on in and do it! I looked down at my hands as they started to shake.

12 LUST

A fortnight passed since the night Rob had gone astray, yet still he swore he had been in the bathroom. I spent a night at Renae's place, venting about my feelings and worries. She engrained into me that I was over thinking the night, as maybe he had been in the cubicle at the time I walked over to check, and maybe while I was wandering around looking for him he had come out and couldn't find me himself. I felt somewhat at ease after chatting with her, and also shared with her my confrontation with Absolute, along with the whole repulsive seediness which the scene was infested with. She tried to justify the fact that Para-dice'etcya was perhaps the only place for some of its patrons where they felt safe and truly able to be themselves. She said that when they were at the club their endeavours and personalities were most probably heightened due to feeling restricted in everyday society. I suppose it made sense, as I too felt I could relax when I entered Para-dice'ectya. I never felt judged or different inside the club. But it didn't excuse the seediness. It didn't excuse every time I was groped or felt up on the dance floor.

The fortnight ahead saw multiple nights out. Rob made sure I felt secure, staying with me at all times, and asking me to come with him when he had to go to the bathroom. Gathered with our group one evening, I cuddled into his arm where I felt safe and content. After two weeks of reassurance, I felt a lot better about Rob. One night while we were at his place snuggled up on the couch, I asked what we were and if we had become an item.

"What do you mean?" Rob asked, pulling out of our snuggled position to look at me.

"I mean, are we official? Are you my boyfriend?" I asked.

"Well, we're dating, but I wouldn't go that far just yet, babe," he said.

"But we are exclusive, aren't we?" I asked. Rob hesitated. "You're not seeing anyone else, are you?"

"Mikey," he paused. "I've been in a few monogamous relationships in the past. I've been hurt and, I won't lie, I've hurt people too," he said. I started to fret. "I think it's better if we just see where this goes and not put a label on it. Let's not ruin the fun of the mystery."

"So what are you saying? You want to see other guys?" I asked.

"No, no. I'm not going to go out of my way to see other guys. I just don't want us putting a label on something so soon," he explained. I sighed. "What, Michael? What's wrong?"

"It's just... I think I'm falling in love with you," I said. Rob wrapped his arms around me and snuggled me.

"I love you too, babe," he said casually, and it was left at that. I went to bed with an unsettled feeling in my gut, and felt somewhat insecure, again. Although he said he loved me, it felt more casual – when I said it I had genuinely meant it.

*

The next morning I woke up with Rob, and I got ready for the day, next to his gorgeous naked body. I felt so lucky to be with someone so dreamy, but his words had begun to make me feel uncertain. I found myself asking how long it would last. Once we readied ourselves for the day, we got into his car. He had to go to work, while I had plans to catch up with Andrew. Conveniently, my plans were in the city, not too far from Rob's work. He parked the car, kissed me goodbye, and we went our separate ways.

"Hi Andrew," I shouted, as I walked to where we had agreed to meet, in West Perth.

"Hey dude. What's up?"

"Nothing much. Robs just gone off to work," I said. Andrew and I walked into Northbridge, along James Street, the main club strip. It looked so different in the day without the stumbling drunk girls in heels and beefed up deros. Andrew and I found a spot to grab some bubble tea, and walked about aimlessly while we caught up on each other's lives. There were a few exhibitions on display which we looked at in the Cultural Centre, and we caught some buskers, which entertained us for a while. Before we knew it, our stomachs were calling for food.

"Let's surprise Rob for Lunch!" I suggested. Andrew agreed, and we walked back towards Rob's workplace. On our way, I apologised for the night I had left Andrew and Renae in the cab. He seemed to understand and forgive, as best friends usually do, but at the same time made it known he was pretty disappointed in me that night. He suddenly grabbed my shoulder to hold me back from walking any further.

"Uh, Michael," he said. I stopped. "Isn't that Rob?" I looked ahead and, sure enough, it was. He was standing across the other side of the road, holding hands and talking with another guy. They looked close. "Don't think too much of it, man. Maybe it's a friend? A close brother…"

suggested Andrew. But before I had a chance to contemplate, Rob leaned

in and kissed the guy. "Italian brothers?" Andrew said, humorously. "Fuck.

I'm sorry man. This is a joke, not again." Rob and the other man continued

to kiss.

"I don't think so," I said. My heart felt as if it had stopped beating and

froze solid. It felt like I filled with a rainforest of tears, with not one tear

able to escaped. I filled with so much emotion and anxiety. Not again,

indeed. Not a'fucking'gain! Then, a sudden pain hit my forehead.

"Ahhh!" I shouted. I held my head and kneeled over the ground as my

vision began to fuzz, and then dropped to the floor.

I woke up on the back seat of Rob's car. He was driving, with Andrew

in the front passenger seat.

"Where are we going?" I asked.

"Michael, you're up. How do you feel? Are you okay?" Rob asked.

"I said, where are we going?"

"The hospital. We're taking you to the hospital," said Andrew.

"No, take me home," I said.

"Not going to happen," said Rob. I sat up and stared at Rob through the rear vision mirror.

"Take me home. Nowww!" I screamed. Rob stayed silent, as he lost control of the car for a moment. But quickly regained control of the steering wheel. Oncoming traffic honked at us.

"Okay buddy. We'll take you home. Turn around, Rob," said Andrew. Rob hesitated, looking at Andrew. "Just do it."

The drive back home was silent. If either Rob or Andrew started to speak, I asked them to be quiet. As Rob turned onto my street, he slowed down a few hundred meters before reaching my parents' house and asked Andrew if he'd give us a moment. Andrew looked at me, but I nodded to assure him I was okay with it, and as such he got out of the car. Rob unclipped his seatbelt and turned around to face me.

"Michael, what you saw…" he began to speak.

"I know what I saw," I said. I was filled with heartache, which was becoming fuelled with fury. I was done with Rob. Absolutely, done.

"He's just…"

"Some guy," I said, "Someone you don't feel anything for? I don't need to know who. You told me yourself – we're not a couple we're just enjoying the mystery. Well I'm done with mystery!" Full of angst, I got out of the car and slammed the door before walking up to Andrew. Rob drove up to us and rolled down his window.

"I will call you," he said. I didn't respond. As he drove off, I looked at Andrew.

"We're going clubbing tonight," I said.

"That sounds like the greatest plan you've had all day," said Andrew, filled with encouragement.

That night, after heading back to my place to get ready, Andrew and I hopped in a cab. Sprayed with cologne and my hair neatly slicked back, my own scent had me aroused for what the night may bring. Having already had a few pre-club drinks, Andrew and I were a tad on the tipsy side.

"Are you suuuuuuure they're going to let me in?" asked Andrew.

"Trust me. I've been hitting this place with Rob for months. The bouncers know me like the back of their hand. I haven't been asked for ID once!" I said, reassuring him. As the cab pulled up to the venue, we paid the driver and got out of the car as we giggled, having dropped a bit of change trying to pay in our tipsy state. We walked around the corner to the front entrance, where a bouncer I'd previously had a few tipsy chats with greeted us.

"MIKEY! My boy! How's things?" he asked. I walked closer and swiped his hand then formed a fist as we knuckled each other.

"Can't complain, can't complain," I replied.

"This guy with you?" he asked, pointing to Andrew.

"Yeah, this is Andrew. He's my best bud," I said.

"Here for a boy-licious time are we?" he asked, winking at Andrew.

"Oh no, no. I'm his token straight boy – I'm out for the fag hags," responded Andrew. The bouncer laughed.

"Shame, for the guys," he said, laughing. "All right boys, in you go!" He waved us in. As we walked through, I jumped in excitement.

"See? I told you, man! I've got your back!" I squealed, excitedly. We ran with energy, almost jumping from our skin. Andrew was thrilled, being in a nightclub at seventeen years old was just outrageous to him. He loved it, he didn't care that it was a gay club. He just cared that he was with his bestest buddy in the whole wide world.

"What do you want to drink?" I asked.

"Nah, dude. Let me get this one," said Andrew.

"Andrew, I insist. My parents give me a pretty generous allowance. They can afford it. What do you want?"

"Aaaaaalright," he agreed. "I'll have an energy drink with vodka." I ordered the same, and we walked to the lounge area at the back of the club, lit with a dull pink which shone against maroon padded walls. As Andrew chatted, I zoned out for a moment, looking around at who walked by and who might show interest – I was ready to get the fuck over Rob. I was ready to have a bit of fun. As I looked around, one very mysterious boy with dark hair, black eyeliner, dark shades of clothing and a silver lip piercing looked me up and down as he walked across the room and then out to the beer garden. I looked back at Andrew with a smirk of confidence on my face and took a sip from my drink.

"So, what do you think?" asked Andrew. I sipped my drink for a moment, needing time to think, not taken in what he'd asked straight away.

"I think it's time to dance, that's what I think," I said, skulling my drink and slamming my glass down on the table. I stood and grabbed Andrew's upper arm to pull him up with me.

"Come on, man," I said. He followed.

We walked out to the beer garden where the mysterious boy had walked, and stood with a cigarette between two of his fingers, and placed his lips around the bud as he inhaled. He drew the cigarette away from his lips, blew the smoke out from his mouth and looked over at me, with a cool casual confidence, then winked my way. I smiled, awkwardly, then turned around to Andrew.

"What do I do?" I asked him.

"What do you mean, what do you do?" he asked.

"The guy over there. He winked at me, and he's cute. I've never picked a guy up before. Nott in a club." I explained. Andrew rolled his eyes.

"It's like this," he said, grabbing my shirt and taking me over.

"Hi guys. I'm Andrew and this is my friend, Michael, who's recently gone through a bit of a rough patch with a guy he's been seeing. We're looking for a circle to hang with," said Andrew. The mysterious guy was stood in a circle with three women. They seemed nice enough, as each greeted us with a smile. One of them was a rather large girl with an outfit which draped off her body loosely with a bright red bow in her hair and short dark bob. The other two were ditzy, and they wore low-cut bright coloured tank-tops with their cleavage exposed. Both with bangs. One with blonde hair and the other with black.

"Hi guys. How are you?" asked one of the girls.

"Yeah, what's happening tonight?" asked the other one.

"You dumb fucks. This guy's just told you his friend's out cause of a rough patch. They're out to get wasted and dance – ain't that right, boys?" asked the big girl. I liked her, she had attitude. The mysterious boy continued to smoke his cigarette, watching us in silence, as if sussing us out. I had a quick glance at him as he turned back to face the girls. The glance was enough to make me certain that this was the guy I wanted to make me forget about Rob tonight.

As the night went on, the girls with bangs had introduced themselves as Lisa and Zalia. The big girl had introduced herself as Amy, and the mysterious boy as Reece, saying that he wasn't much for conversation.

"I'm an observer," said Reece, looking at me with a sense of seduction about him. He smiled. Andrew started to enaged with the girls as he bumped me towards Reece. The girls thought Andrew was the cutest thing and the four of them started to flirt.

"Come on," said Reece. "We're going to the dance floor." He waved goodbye to the others and stuck his fingers in the back pocket of my trousers, dragging me along with him. I looked at Andrew as I left with a large grin planted on my face.

On the dance floor, Reece and I began to sway as he held his hands on my waist. In the darkness, the light caught his eyes as they moved, revealing an intriguingly entrancing green.

"So what do you do?" Reece asked.

"I've actually recently graduated from school. I'm not quite sure what I..." I began to speak.

"Bored now," Reece interrupted, as he pulled me into his body. Our chests started rubbing against each other as he gripped the back of my hair to viciously and forcefully make out with me. Kissing him was not the same as I had felt with other guys, it was aggressive, but it was certainly exhilarating and boy did I smile between kisses – indulging in the moment. We continued to move on the dance floor, our bodies sliding up against one another. I slid my hands up underneath his shirt, and I felt his smooth body and light chest hair. Reece continued to ravage his hands through my hair and began biting my lip. He then arched my head away from him and started to suck on my neck. I had never had a hickey before, but I god damn loved the feeling of it. I felt as if he was sucking away all the stress and tension from my body. We must have remained on the dance floor for at least an hour, pulling at each other's clothes, biting each other's necks, lifting each other's shirts and leaving hickeys all over each others necks, pecs and fronts of our shoulders. It was pure ecstasy, but one hundred per cent lust. The girls came running up to us, tugging at Reece's shirt.

"Reece, we've got to go. Amy's not feeling well," Lisa said. Reece looked at them, and then back to me.

"I'm their ride," he said. And before I could pin him back down, he stepped away and left the dancefloor. Andrew ran up to me.

"Far out, dude. What the hell did he do to you?" Andrew asked, looking at the bite marks on my neck. "He's a bloody vampire!"

"Oh, Drew, you have no idea! He's like a vampire! I feel incredible – invincible!" For the rest of the night Andrew and I mucked about. We danced up a storm, childishly plucked hair from people's heads and run off, and made absolute fools of ourselves with dorky moves and funny gestures. Good times. Really, good times. It felt like it had given me the playtime I never got to have a child. Always looking out for my mother. Never with any friends. I let go completely and just played around absolutely ridiculously with Andrew. This place became my new haven. Before it became hell.

13 INSPIRATION

The night I had bit, rubbed and slid my body against Reece, I'd felt

motions in my body I rarely felt again. It was a pretty spontaneous and all-

consuming night. Rebelling from Rob. It's so odd that at times in life you

can feel so on top of the world and adventurous, and then other times you

feel like absolute scum below the earth – utterly worthless. Having sat and

thought back on my life, remembering times when I had been happy, I had

to stop kidding myself. That time was over. Standing up from my chair at

my dresser, I wander out to the kitchen. *Tonight is the night.* I open the top

kitchen drawer, pushing utensils aside to grab a large kitchen knife, which I

take out and carry back to my dressing room. I pack my bag with the usual;

feather bowers, spare sets of stockings, a few change of wigs and some

outfit changes, nestling the knife in amongst it all. Continuing to push

through with the remaining energy I could muster, I sit back down at my

dresser, take a deep breath and exhale. Opening the drawer to the dresser in front of me, I pick out a deep purple eye-shadow, ready to apply the final touches to my face for the very last time. *I'm doing this.* The purple reminds me of the hickeys I had on my neck the day after my lustrous encounter with Reece.

I remember the next morning, waking up in my bed and walking to the bathroom to find the cream colour of my skin infested with dark purple blotches. Walking out to breakfast that morning was an experience, as I tried to cover them up with the collar of my shirt. Not that it worked. Sitting at the table eating a bowl of cereal, mum came up behind me and spotted a mark below the hairline of my neck.

"Are you okay?" she asked.

"Yeah, why?" I asked, confused at the time.

"Your neck. Do you feel alright?"

"Oh, gosh. I don't know what to tell you, mum."

"Oh, I see. So, when do we meet this boy?"

"Um, I don't know what to tell you there either, sorry. We didn't exactly swap numbers," I explained.

"Ha," mum laughed. "Like mother, like son. I had a few of those in my time don't you worry." She sat down across from me. "Just don't be silly. Never bring a stranger home and make sure you don't just go home with anyone." I reassured her, but in my head had a little giggle to myself recalling the moment I had lost my virginity, and when I'd gone home with Rob. That same morning, Rob actually called me. Lying in my room listening to music with nothing better to do, I decided to pick up.

"Hello?" I answered.

"Hi Mikey. How are you doing?" Rob asked.

"Better than ever, actually," I replied.

"Oh, is that so?" Rob responded.

"Yup. How about you?" I asked.

"Not too bad. Just wondering what you're up to?"

"Nothing much. Want to hang?" I asked. Rob paused on the line for a moment.

"Yeah, let's – so long as we're okay?"

"Absolutely," I answered. I wasn't exactly sure what I hoped to achieve by agreeing to meet with him. I certainly didn't want any outcome that would see us get back together. Maybe I just wanted to see him grovel a little. I was feeling pretty confident in myself, maybe even a little reckless.

*

That afternoon I met up with Rob in King's Park. I remember sat on the grass slope looking out across to Perth's small city skyline along the Swan River. How peaceful it looked from afar. As I looked out, I saw Rob approach from the corner of my eye. I got up to greet him as he came forward and embraced me in his arms. He smelled my skin as if I was a soldier that had returned from war. He slid his hand up my shirt and squeezed me tight. I almost just about gave in, feeling like I missed his touch. I didn't. I wouldn't.

"I've missed you," he said. "I've been worried." Rob put his finger underneath my chin to manipulate my face towards his own. He kissed me. "And I've missed that. Being apart from you last night tortured me." He leant back, looking into my eyes. He ran his fingers through my hair, looked back at my eyes and then down to my lips. He flinched, catching glimpse of my hickeys.

"What's this?" asked Rob, stepping back from me and breaking his embrace. I wasn't quite sure what to say, but he continued to talk regardless. "Did you go to Para-dice'etcya last night?"

"So what if I did?"

"Hmm," Rob murmured. "And to think I was worried about you." I didn't understand his annoyance, his attitude towards me didn't seem valid, considering what I caught him hiding the day Andrew and I thought we'd surprise him for lunch. "I'll call you later, okay?"

"What do you mean? You just got here," I said.

"Yeah, and now I'm going," he said as he began to walk backwards and then turned and walked away. I truly could not believe it. As he walked away, I realised that I had caused whatever annoyance or attitude he had just adopted. I began to enjoy the experience; instead of chasing after him or walking off myself, I stood and stared, indulging in what felt like a triumph. I had hurt him, and I liked it. I wished I could have hurt him even more. Have him find *me* with another guy. Yeah, I would have loved to have seen the look on his face.

*

As the weeks went by, I consumed myself within the scene. I clubbed most nights and slept most mornings, never awakening until the early hours of the afternoon. I made pals with Reece's friends Lisa, Zalia and Amy after spotting them out one night and partying with them for a number of nights after that. They had parted ways with Reece, he'd become addicted to drugs, and he'd pushed them away in their efforts to help.

Wrapped up in the scene, I wanted to share it with everyone. It had become my life. I even took mum out with me one night. Yes, I was *that* gay. Andrew dragged his own mother along too. Introducing mum to my world was a fantastic feeling and, when we hit the dance floor, she had a few moves she had previously neglected to share with me herself. I saw a little joy spark in her on that dancefloor. Happy, to be out with her first son. Happy, to have been invited. I felt bad about what I had put her through, and it brought a real smile to my face to see her enjoying herself. One night I called Renae to see if she wanted to get together for a catch-up, and if she'd be interested in coming to the club. It was a quieter night, being mid-week, but she was keen. It really has my haven for a time.

At the club, there were only a couple of punters here and there, it really was a quite night. A few people stood at the bar and a couple of odd groups stood in their own clusters. There were tables and chairs set out in the beer garden with the lack of people to fill it, with a few coloured podium blocks scattered around, which I had been known to hop on and *work it* in my drunker moments. This night, however, the atmosphere was chilled and the DJ played much slower tempo tunes. It was a really intimate surrounding to catch up with Renae. We found a nice pair of chairs and a table up against one of the coloured podiums, which projected a nice ray of blue light and set a relaxed mood.

"How have you been?" I asked. Renae started to cry, but fought to hold back her tears as she spoke.

"He left me," she said. "He left me for some bimbo he met at work – a temp!"

"Oh Renae." I felt horrible for her. She sniffed, and gathered herself.

"It's okay. I'm coming to terms with it but it's been so hard, not having anyone beside me, and not having anyone to come home to," she said. It was a pretty surreal moment, Renae had been with that guy for almost ten-years. Although I had never been with anyone as long as her, I could sympathise with the feeling.

The evening continued with the gossip that had become my life, including the story of Rob and Reece. Renae said she had wondered about Rob for some time, and didn't hold too much respect for him after having snatched me away the night she passed out in the cab. But she hadn't wanted to share her thoughts with me, as she didn't want to influence my relationship with him. We continued to fill each other in on our lives, and having partied so hard of late it was really refreshing to just sit back and relax over a drink with a friend. I felt the rekindling was also due, and it grounded me a little, bringing me back to reality with the realisation that there were other things going on in the world other than drinking, dancing and kissing boys.

At one point in the night, I remember a moment which changed the rest of my life. It is what inspired me to become, Sacrifice, and ultimately created the pathway that led me to pack the kitchen knife in my bag. I remember going to the bar to order Renae and myself another drink, and as I stood waiting for the bartender to serve me, the tunes to the DJ faded. Over the speakers, someone spoke. *And now we're going to take things down a tone with a little number called 'Here's to Life'*. I turned around and, standing on the podium by our table, was a drag queen I had not met before. She was dressed in an elegant light blue dress, which was covered in a light layer of silver glitter which glistened. The queen held a microphone, and her long flowing blonde hair weaved around her face and down her back. She was simply beautiful. A real 'Glenda' the good witch.

A piano started to play over the speakers and, as the song began, the queen brought the microphone up to her mouth. She held herself with such proper posture and the most graceful stance, and then she began to sing the most gorgeous lyrics. *No complaints, and no regrets. I still believe in chasing dreams, and placing bets. For I have learned that all you give, is all you get. So give it alllll you've got.* Or at least, the words appeared to flow from her mouth. However, the voice which came out from the speakers was familiar. I soon realised it was Barbra Streisand. The mic that the drag queen was holding wasn't turned on – she was lip syncing, impeccably.

The barman tapped me on the shoulder and handed me the drinks I'd ordered. With my eyes fixated on the performance of the drag queen, I walked slowly back to my seat. As I approached, Renae took her drink. Before I sat down, the drag queen on the podium beside our table reached below and held her free hand to the side of my face, as she continued to lip sync, *may all your storms be weathered, and all that's good get better. Here's to life. Here's to love. Here's to you.* I stood captivated by her presence, delicate in her movement and emotive in her gestures and expressions. As an instrumental piece of the song started to play, she took her hand from my face and spun ever so delicately around on the podium. She shut her eyes and swayed to the music, as if she felt something from the song true to herself. I sat back down, with my eyes still glued to the performance. As she continued, not only the lyrics of the song, but the way in which she presented it, touched me. I felt goosebumps take over my skin, and tingles take to the inside of me. As I watched the end of her performance, I thought to myself that it was something I could do too. I'd met drag queens, but I'd never seen one perform. I'd always been so wrapped up in the bar, boys and dancing. I had not ever really noticed or considered what a drag performance was or could be. I always saw Absolute around in her fabulous outfits, but never once had I thought to ask her what she actually did or when a show was on. I just thought she wandered the club looking fabulous.

Right then and there, was my inspiration and love for the art of drag, and for what I wanted to do with my life. After the way the performance moved me, and the way it captured my attention with inspiration and admiration, I wanted to make people feel the same way. I wanted to connect with people in the way I just felt. Having dabbled in the arts, I held theatricality, as well as a natural rhythm and a certain technique in movement, but what I didn't have was any experience or skill in make-up. The performer I saw that night looked simply beautiful and soft. Not like the harsh tones of Angelica Absolute. The queens face this night, was like an angel – as if they'd just flown down from heaven.

*

I went home that night, heading to bed with a million thoughts and ideas running through my head. The nights that followed saw me drag all of my mum's albums and CDs out, flicking from track to track to find a song I felt I could deliver, and one I could truly connect with for my first performance. In my room with my stereo turned up, I found a song which really grabbed me, and I began to practice lip syncing it in the mirror. Once I had memorised the words, I practiced performing it over and over again, sneaking a pair of heels from my mum's wardrobe hoping that she wouldn't notice. The heels themselves were too small for me, so I got a pair of scissors and cut a slit down the back of the heel. Each rehearsal came with

more feeling and power, and I was consumed with drive and dedication –
two things of which my life had previously lacked until this point. All it
took was one moment of inspiration, and seeing something I felt I could
aspire to, as until that moment I never had. It was then I knew what I
wanted to do to fulfil my life, and it was *drag*.

*

After a month of rehearsals, I felt ready for my debut performance.
However, I was still lacking the experience in make-up. If I was going to do
this, I was not going to half-heartedly slap on some of my mum's
foundation and lipstick. I wanted it to be perfect, and I wanted to come out
with a bang! I looked up online pictures of drag queens, and there were
many large bright colourful faces, some of which were close to scary with
eyebrows drawn up to the top of their foreheads. But what I wanted was a
nice petite face, which showed the softness I hoped to project and
complemented the persona I wanted to portray. I wasn't going into this
industry to be loud and proud, but rather to express myself, use it as a
creative platform, and allow others to admire the art and relate on some
level.

Knowing what needed to be done to complete my transition into the
drag industry, I approached the one queen I knew, Miss Angelica Absolute.
She was not my most favourite character, and although she had tried one

on with me the night I was looking for Rob, she was the head queen of the club. If I was going to learn anything, I was going to learn it from her.

14 THE CREATION

One night I went out to the club by myself, on a mission. Not filled with alcohol or there to hook-up, the atmosphere felt different. I walked around looking for Absolute. Making my way through the crowds, I reached the beer garden where I saw her ahead, towering over everyone else with a large blonde beehive wig. I walked over and said hi.

"Well hello, young man," she said, greeting me warmly. "What can I do for you?"

"I have a favour to ask you, actually," I said.

"I told you, Michael, any time," said Absolute.

"Actually, it was about drag," I said, ignoring her sleazy response. Her eyes widened with interest, and she extended her arm to me.

"You're interested in starting drag?"

"Well, yeah."

"Let's walk and talk," she said, guiding me beside her as she walked us through the building crowd. I explained to her the love I had felt for the art after the performance I had seen with Renae. Absolute informed me that the queen I had seen was called *Panache*. She was a drag queen over from the eastern states, who had actually grown up locally in Perth, and was working a few nights a week for the next couple of months while she was in town looking after some family matters.

"She's well versed in the drag scene. You'd really have to hit it hard before you came close to mastering the art at her level," Absolute said. That didn't deter me – I was prepared to work hard for it. I wanted to perfect the art of drag more than anything I'd ever wanted ever. I had never been so sure of anything in my life. And with that, Absolute and I exchanged numbers and arranged a time for her to do my first drag face. To teach me the tricks of the trade – by brush.

*

The afternoon I arrived at Absolute's house I was a little nervous, but ecstatic at the same time. I brought the CD with my track on it, and the pair of shoes I had been practicing in. It wasn't too hard to find her place – it was only one bus trip away from my place. I arrived just before sundown.

Prior to walking up the driveway, I stood back and double checked the address against the one I had in my phone. I looked back at the street sign, and then at the number on the letter box. It was indeed the right house, and it was phenomenal. The letterbox alone was a masterpiece, a modern sculpture with a slit to insert mail lit with red light. I walked down the drive and, as I approached the front door, admiring the house, rendered with a deep grey-tone. The doorbell was illuminated by red as well, set beside two large double doors. I pressed the doorbell and only had to wait for a few moments. The door swung wide open. Inside was a male with swept light brown hair, a mustard-coloured turtle neck and grey skinny jeans. He was very cute, with a dainty yet familiar smile.

"Hi, my name's Michael. I'm here to see Angelica," I said, introducing myself. The man in front of me laughed.

"Are you now?" he asked. I stood uncertainly. The man laughed again. "It's me, silly. Angelica!" It was too. She was incredibly different out of costume and make-up. The smile I recognised was certainly hers, but the lips were thinner and the cheekbones and jaw seemed entirely different.

"Come in, you silly sausage," he said. As I entered, he reintroduced himself as Harry. I suppose I had never considered what he might look like out of costume or what his actual name was. He had always just been, Angelica. He took me through the front of the house. It was filled with decorative ornaments, and had high ceilings which made the house seem even more spacious.

"This way," he guided me through to what he called the activity room. It was actually his bedroom, and a large one at that. Opposite his bed was a large Victorian style dressing table, with a large mirror and wings either side which held foam head pieces with styled wigs. On either side of the dresser were long racks with his collection of costumes.

"Take a seat, doll," he said. "Fancy a drink?"

"I'm okay," I said.

"Well, don't mind if I do. An old gal like me needs her night cap!" said Harry. I sat down and looked around the room while he went off to collect a drink for himself. The room was deep purple, with a large black velvet bedhead. To the side of the bed was a large black set of drawers, with photo frames holding pictures of himself and another man. When he returned to the room, I asked him who the other man in the photos was. He said his name was Ric, and that Ric was his fiancé. "Well, as legally as he can be anyway," he added.

"Oh nice. Why is he never out at the clubs?" I asked.

"Oh, Ric isn't really into the whole, scene thing. He just leaves

Absolute to it. But he engages in quite the few after parties don't you worry your little pants about that," he said, as he sat down in front of the dresser with me and pulled out a large silver metal box. "You'll need a good sturdy make-up case like this yourself, my dear," he said.

Opening the box from the middle, out popped two ends from either side. "I give you Angelica Absolute!" he said, revealing a box full of powders, eyeshadows, lipsticks and all kinds of makeup. Harry began to talk to me about the shades of colours he preferred, the ones he used most, and why. What colours signified. What went well together and what did not. "It's all about the impression you want to leave, darling."

He began to compare the colour of my skin to colour tones of foundation he had in his box.

"So have you thought of a name?" he asked, rummaging through his box for a selection of items as he lined them up along the dresser.

"No, actually. I haven't," I said.

"Well, a queen's got to have a name. What is it you're wanting to get out of this, doll? Who is it that you want to be?" Harry asked. I thought for a while. I knew all this, but putting it into a name was difficult. As I thought, something inside me clicked.

"Sacrifice," I answered.

"Pow," responded Harry. "Very nice. Why so?"

"It's pretty. I like it, and it stands for what I've done to get here."

"That's deep, my dear," said Harry, as he brushed his hands. "Right, are you ready to get started?!"

"As ready as I'll ever be," I replied certainly.

Over the next few hours I sat and watched through the mirror as Harry applied various products to my face. Starting with a wax, he pasted down my eyebrows and smoothed them over with a plastic tool shaped similarly to a bread and butter knife. He padded it down with powder to set the wax, and then started to apply foundation to my skin and over the top of it, which had created a flat surface and made me look like I had no eyebrows at all. Once he finished the layer of foundation, I looked at myself in the mirror.

"I look like a cancer patient," I said. Harry laughed.

"Just you wait – there's much more to come," said Harry.

Continuing with my face, now a canvas of one tone, he began to highlight areas of my face with a lighter foundation. He highlighted underneath my eyes, a thin strip down the top of my nose and on either side of my jaw. He began to blend it into the darker foundation with a sponge. As the next step, he got a brown eyeliner pencil and held my head, beginning to draw a line from where my eyebrow naturally started, and then continued to draw it up and over creating a feminine arch. Harry started to fill parts of the line, and eventually it looked as if they were my real eyebrows. Next, he used a black and brown shadow around my eyelids, making sure my eyelid remained tan. After smoking the colours together, he drew flicks with black liquid eyeliner along the edge of my lids to the ends of each eye. He filled my real lashes with mascara, and then applied larger fake ones on top. At this point he turned my seat away from the mirror to face him.

Facing Harry, I closed my eyes and relaxed in the moment. He asked me to open my mouth slightly, and I felt a wet brush caress my lips, both top and bottom. I felt strokes of a large dry brush against my cheekbones, which relaxed me even more, and soon each stroke sent me into a daze.

"All right. Before you can look, we need to get you a dress and a hair style," said Harry.

"I brought shoes," I said. "They're just down there." I pointed, where I had placed them when I entered the room.

"Doll, if you're dragging up, you're dragging up. Those heels have seen hard days. I will lend you a pair."

Searching through his costumes, he pulled out a pink sparkly sequin gown and laid it on the bed. Then he looked up at his wigs with uncertainty, hitting his chin back and forth with his index finger.

"Oh, I know just the one. Now take off your shirt and trousers," he instructed. I sat for a moment longer. "Come on, don't be shy now. Take them off! How are you going to wear a bra and tuck your bits back like that?"

I stood a little hesitantly, but took my clothing off and stood in my underwear.

"Here, turn around," said Harry, holding a bra. As I turned, he placed the bra in front of me and pulled it back behind my back, clipping it in place. As he walked back to the dresser I looked down at the bra, squishing my skin together to make it look like cleavage.

"You don't quite have enough flab for that to work, doll. Here, put these in," he said, tossing me two pairs of bunched socks.

"Socks?" I asked.

"Darn straight! Nice and firm, just how you want them," he said. I put the socks into my bra. Harry walked behind me, grabbing my shoulders.

"You okay, doll?" he asked.

"Yes." I answered, as he ran his hand down my back and into my underwear.

"Now I'm just going to help you out a little here," he said. Harry's hand passed down my butt crack and underneath me where he grabbed my penis and balls. I closed my eyes and stood still. "Nice," he whispered. Not quite sure what to respond with, I said thanks with my eyes closed tight. He slowly moved his fingers, as if he had a pair of Chinese stress balls in his hands. "Tucking is an art of its own, my dearie," said Harry. He pulled my penis and balls back softly between my legs. In a way, it felt pleasant, but I was resistant and stood still. "Hold your legs tight," instructed Harry. I pushed my thighs together and opened my eyes as he let go of my genitals. "Now you're a woman!" he said.

I pulled the elastic of my underwear outwards and looked down in front of me with my penis tucked away, it really did look like I had nothing there.

"But how does it stay?" I asked.

"Each to their own. There are many ways, but it's up to you which works best. Some duct tape, some just wear extremely tight underwear over a few layers of tight stockings. There's even underwear with a string and socket available to keep it pulled back, but it's ultimately what's comfortable for you." He started to dress me, handing me a thick pair of stockings, helping me zip up the dress, and finally asked me to shut my eyes while he fit the wig. With my eyes still shut, he held me from behind and moved me in front of the mirror. "You can open your eyes now," he said.

Opening my eyes slowly, I looked in the mirror and stared. Before me, I didn't see myself. Instead, I saw Sacrifice, and she was glorious. I stared in complete and utter astonishment. I raised my hand to my face, and touched what looked like flawless skin, and then felt where my hair sat just below my ears. A short blonde curled wig, I just about looked like Marilyn Munroe.

"You're an artist," I said to Harry.

"No, you were an exceptional canvas. You've got the most petite face for it," he said. I continued to stare at myself, in love with what I saw as I tilted my head from side to side, admiring the creation that was before me.

"So, you said you had a number to show me," said Harry.

"Ah, yes." I headed over to where my old heels were in the corner of the room with the CD up against them. I picked it up and handed it to Harry.

"Come on then, follow me," he said. I followed Harry, in an exquisite pair of his gem-encrusted heels, which were much more comfortable than the ones I had been wearing. He led me to a large living space across from his opulent and stylish kitchen, and placed the disc into his CD player. "Okay, let's see what you've got," said Harry, sitting on a red leather couch. He picked up the remote, and pressed play. I took a deep breath, and let out a slow exhale. The music began, and as the lyrics started, so did I, in full swing. I felt the beats within me, and I performed as if I was on a stage for thousands of people. I felt every beat as it hit, lip synching to 'Song for the Lonely' by Cher. *When you're standing on the edge of nowhere, there's only one way up so your heart's got to go there. Through the darkest night, see the light shine bright. When heroes fall, in love or war, they live forever.* As I continued to perform, my body filled with tingles, and I felt as if I'd found my true calling.

*

One year later, I was on the stage at Para-dice'ectya as their resident hostess and showgirl, performing my song as part of their tribute to the stars show. Each and every time I performed it, I felt it. I connected with audiences, stayed true to myself and loved each and every moment of it. *This is a song, for the lonely. Can you hear me tonight? For the broken-hearted, battle-scarred I'll be by your side. And this is a song, for the lonely, when your dreams won't come true. Can you hear this prayer? Cause someone's there for you.*

Although I loved the song, by this time I had compiled a nice set of song lists for performances, but I always brought back my debut number, as it stood for who I was. What I stood for. Why I was doing it and what I had been through. My parents had become my number one fans, attending most performances and cheering me on from the back of the gay infested crowds. They totally stood out, but they loved it. Even dad, as proud of me up there in heels as when I was accepted into Lumier. Six months earlier I had competed in a competition called *Queen of Para-dice*, and it was then I began to collect a nice little following for myself. Before that it had been amateur drag nights, a kind of open mic night for drag. But on taking out Queen of Para-dice, I was offered resident work at the club for my reigning year. The moment I was announced as the winner my legs turned to jelly, and my chest filled with butterflies. I had never won anything before yet alone been encouraged and applauded for it. I remembered back to the moment I witnessed Simon and Natalie accepting their crowns at the School Ball, and how I aspired to be as popular and cherished one day. That day had certainly come. Working hard, and being true to myself, I had become the 'Queen of Para-dice'. Little did I know at the time, what it would cost me, to keep hold of those reigns.

15 PARA-DICE WITH SACRIFICE

Living the dream, I had hit a form of stardom within the scene. Each time I stepped out in my heels, I was greeted and welcomed warmly, offered drinks upon arrival and, asked to be in almost every selfie taken at the club. Sacrifice was a hit, and she was adored by her fans. The trouble started, with the fact that not everyone was a fan of Sacrifice. Ima Nomans, most certainly was not. Her presence truly left a cold shiver run down my spine. Anyone's spine really. She was followed by a group of sheep-like queens who were just as horrid. Like the nasty popular girls at school, in a pack.

Their names were Sharon Husbands, Pablo Va and Bella De'Ball. Sharon was a club kid, new to the scene and a girly thing. Often dressed in outfits which resembled the days of the Spice Girls, and she styled her wigs in piggy and pony tails. Pablo was pretty much a mini Ima, always out to stare people down, strut through the club and step on anyone's toes that she could. But not just step, *SQUASH!* Bella, however, was a quieter queen. You could never quite read her. Bella mostly kept to herself, but always hung on to the group that Absolute and I referred to as the I-squad. Little had I known at that time, Absolute was closer to the I-squad than she let on. But if I think back enough, I can recall some tell-tale signs. It was no surprise to learn the two faces of Angelica in the end. The surprise, was the horrific act I ended up catching her in.

At the highest point of my career in drag, a film production company had approached the club to produce a late-night local community talk show, and they had requested me as the presenter. I was absolutely thrilled. My career in drag had gone from competition winner, to resident showgirl, to hostess of the club – under the wing of Absolute, of course – to local community television show presenter! It was a humorous time for me. I remember how the I-squad and, groupies of theirs who previously gave me the cold shoulder, suddenly began to give me the light of day. They wanted to let me know that if I ever needed a guest they'd be happy to come on the show. It was almost laughable, seeing their hunger for attention, groveling to someone they'd never once batted an eyelid in the direction of. Tall poppy syndrome, on being crowned Queen of Para-dice, had most certainly taken effect. Not that any of them had ever been to pleasant to me in my amateur days either.

The show was a sensation. Every Saturday night to reel punters in earlier and, encourage them to spend money over the bar, the set was based in the padded lounge across from the bar, with a rope divider between myself, my guests and the camera men. The general public could stand behind the rope and watch the show live if they wished. Management of Para-dice were overjoyed with the attention it got, as it brought all sorts of people to the club, and bred real new life. They were particularly thrilled with the 'Patrons of Para-dice' segment, where two roving reporters went out into the crowds with the camera and questioned or played novel games with the punters. The segment was popular with hens nights, birthdays and anniversaries, and it drew people into the club for their chance to get on tv, but it was also a great opportunity for the gays to get their five minutes of fame. Oh, how they loved that.

The show itself was called 'Para-dice with Sacrifice'. Each week I featured a special guest in the lounge area who I opened the show with. I discussed who they were in the scene, what position they held in the community, and their inspirations and motivations to become who they were and the part that they played in the community. The guests ranged from gay politicians, gay-friendly business owners, visiting celebrities and gay icons and, of course, drag queens. I had a ball when I was interviewing the guests but, when it was an interview with another queen, I was always wary. I could almost sense the resentment as I interviewed some of them. The desire to take to the seat *I* had been offered. However, there were the odd lovely ones, and I enjoyed watching their responses as they beamed with excitement and showed genuine gratitude for being on the show.

One week in particular, I was a truly anxious mess. It was the week leading up to the night I was scheduled to interview the intolerable, Ima Nomans 'the Vision'. It was a shame that I let her affect me so, as this was *my* show and *I* was the presenter. I had a ball with previous guests, and it was usually a laugh a second on the show. In fact, when I had the grand Angelica Absolute herself on the show, the recording was positively enjoyable every second - no matter the two faced bitch I found her in the end to be. Angelica had always been pleasant to me really. Seedy, but pleasant. Ima, was cold. She lacked empathy or care factor. Thinking ahead, to Ima, I was preparing for hell. I felt like the primary school boy again, ready to be the bud of the joke. The show was LIVE, and I was ready for Ima to pull, *anything*.

When the night finally came I took my seat on set, dressed in what I hoped was my best attire and wig. I kept it classic, a silver sparkling sequin gown with a neat and tidy blonde beehive. I could sense the judgment onto me, before Ima even took her seat, being interviewed by the queen who was on stage two seconds and became a tv presenter for the community. As a crew member powdered my nose, Ima approached in a true GaGa-esque outfit with an extraordinary headpiece. The costume shone in the light, a stretchy metallic lycra covered in shattered mirror. Her headpiece was not much larger than a fascinator, but stood out being made up of wire and shattered glass which rose from the crown of her head and curved down to cover her right eye as if it were a fringe. As she reached the set and turned around for one of the production crew to fit a mic to her, I saw her repulsive back fat droop over the corset which held her feminine hourglass shape in place, repulsive like her presence. The thing was, I didn't care about backfat. I didn't care about someone's weight. Ima, just *made* it repulsive. She could have been stick thin and I would have found *that* repulsive on her. Though she certainly dressed well to distract, with headpieces, large shoulder pads and unique accessories.

My anxiety grew as she entered, the crew lifting the robe for her entry to the set. For the first time ever, our eyes actually connected as she walked towards me. I smiled, unsure of what else to do. She didn't smile back, and took her seat beside me while brushing herself off. I started to sweat, with drips forming on the side of my ear and the top of my forehead. I dabbed the drips away, knowing I had to do something to cut the tension.

"So," I piped up and spoke. "That's an incredible costume, Ima."

"Well, you know, got to bring out the big guns for television. Wouldn't want to be caught in a flimsy sequin gown," she said, and I was almost certain that she was referring to my own garment. I didn't let her get me down though, as I was proud of my gown and I looked damn good in it. It was made up of quality sequins, heavier than their weight in gold with a large train which trailed around me seated, as if a large puddle of water surrounded my feet, glistening. The top of the dress which sat just below my cleavage was sewn with crystals, large and small, which started heavy and scattered themselves down the dress. I'm sure I could have worn the exact same outfit as her, with better quality fabrics and accessories, and still have been accused of wearing flimsy attire.

The show must go on, I thought, and so it did. Moments before we went to air, after sitting in silence, Ima turned to me and looked me up and down.

"Don't fuck it up," she said, as if she were my superior. Her attitude really started to get to me, no matter how hard I'd tried to resist letting it. Ima looked towards the camera. I stared at her unimpressed, as her face changed in an instant from sour to a bright and smiley queen as the crew counted down.

"Aaaand, action!" shouted one of the crewmen. My mind began to fuzz. *God damn it – not now!* My head started to throb and rattle, as if a bag of popcorn was cooking and about to burst. The pressure was unbearable. I blacked out to wake in hospital. Again. I looked around me, no-one was beside me this time. As I looked around, sounds which beeped consistently pierced my head, as if a screwdriver was making its way through my nose to the center of my eyebrows. Twisting with each beep. I squinted and, with my vision slightly blurred, got out from bed, my head still throbbing. I held the palms of my hands to either side of my temples. I pushed down hard as if to compact and segregate the pain. But it did not work. I stood from my bed and started to wander around, confused and in agony. I walked out from my ward and into a long hall with fluorescent lights which seemed to me like they were flickering, unsure if I was just hallucinating. Walking down the hall, a nurse asked if I was okay.

"I'm fine!" I shouted, pushing her away with my arm.

"Sir, I mean ma'am, you need to go back to your ward," she said. *Ma'am? Am I still in drag? I must have horribly-smeared makeup and hair.* Ignoring the nurse, I continued to walk. Ahead of me I saw Andrew running towards me, not sure if it was really him or not. My mind played tricks on me as his head stretched bigger and then back smaller, fluctuating as he came close.

"Michael, are you all right?" asked Andrew, holding me up with his arms either side of me.

"I'm going to throw up," I said, as my stomach turned.

"Nurse! Where's the bathroom?" Andrew shouted. The nurse came rushing up and together they led me. Before I made it inside, I started to vomit.

"We're almost there, Michael," said Andrew. But before we even entered, I blacked out again.

*

The next thing I remember is waking up in my own bed at home. I couldn't remember how I had got there, or who had taken me out of hospital, but I was home. I lay in bed trying to think back and remember for a while, but nothing came to me. Lifting the covers off me, I slipped out of bed and walked to my wardrobe, wrapping my dressing gown around me. I opened the door to my room and walked out to the kitchen.

"Hi sweetheart," said mum, cutting up vegetables at the kitchen counter. "How are you?" I walked up to a stool by the bench to sit on it.

"What happened?" I asked.

"We were awfully worried about you. You weren't very chatty when you got home."

"When I got home?" I asked, still not recalling anything beyond passing out at the hospital.

"Yeah, sweetie. You were very dreary. You certainly weren't yourself,"
she explained. Not wanting to let on that I hadn't remembered, I just said I
was tired and had a rough night. She continued to cut up vegetables while
she listened to me, with a concerned and caring look on her face, and she
gathered the cut vegetables with her hands to put them in a pot.

*

I called Andrew later that night. He explained that after I passed
out at the hospital, all of the nurses in the ward rushed to me, and once
they had me back in bed he had stayed overnight to look out for me. The
scary thing was that he said I had woken the next morning, but had not
spoken a word. I just laid in the bed blankly. When he dropped me home,
he just assumed that I had been mad with him for some reason, refusing to
speak with him. I'd been pretty neglectful of him becoming wrapped up in
the scene. I suppose he might of thought he'd been just as neglectful –
though it's pretty hard to reach out to someone when they keep fobbing
you off. At least mum had called to ask him to collect me, as she'd had to
collect dad from the airport. It was nice to speak to him. Still, I couldn't
believe I had blocked out a whole day of my life. The blackouts were one
thing, but this was a whole new level.

*

The next day I received a message from management at the club to come in and chat with them. I turned up on time, and waited nervously on the club strip of Northbridge outside the locked doors of Para-dice'etcya. While the sun glared over me, I leaned against the building with my arms folded, hoping that this episode of mine would not reoccur if management had reorganised the interview with Ima. Down the road, Rudy, the manager, walked towards me. He held files and papers to his chest with one hand, while the other scavenged in his pocket. Pulling out a set of keys, he arrived at the entrance and unlocked the door, greeting me hectically.

"Is everything all right?" I asked.

"Yes, fine, just a late start," he said, as he unlocked and opened the door. Making our way to the office, he asked how I had been and if I was feeling better. I assured him I was okay, even if I wasn't all that great at the time. We sat down at his desk, him behind it and me in front, while he placed his files and papers down to take his sunglasses off. Rudy was a lovely man, a genuine character who always listened to a reply with interest. He began to tidy up his desk and put some papers and folders to the side. He placed his hands on the desk in front of him, clasped together as if I were about to be told off by a school principal. Something was off about the situation, and my nerves began to rise.

"Sacrifice, my dear. It was a rather scary night for all of us a few nights ago," said Rudy.

"Yes indeed," I said in agreement.

"The thing is, nowhere on your paperwork does it mention you have any kind of condition. Yet, a chat with the hospital staff let me in on what you have" he said.

"Yes, I'm so sorry. It's not something I like to share," I said.

"The nurses informed me that it's a rather extreme condition. You neglected to inform us Michael, and that could have held us liable if anything serious had occurred as a result of that night. Do you hear what I'm saying?" asked Rudy.

"Yes, I do," I answered unenthusiastically, as I became fairly certain of where he was leading with this.

"Sac, Sac, Sac. I love you. I adore you. But I'm afraid word spreads pretty fast, and, well, I'm just going to come straight out and say it. The directors got wind of it and have asked me to let you go."

Sat in the chair in front of him, I almost fell into a ball of tears. My anxiety rose high, knowing that I would lose all that I had built and all that I had worked so hard to get. What's worse is that I instantly thought of what the other queens would be saying and the glory that they would feel when they found out I had been dismissed.

"Rudy, you can't do this," I said, as I began to tear. "This place, this show, and Sacrifice, they're my life. If anything, they are the only things that have kept me going. If you do this to me, if you let me go, I don't know what else I'll do." Rudy looked at me with eyes as if to say *I want to help you, but my hands are tied.* I couldn't believe it. If I was being dismissed, sure there were odd pop-up gay nights here and there. But this was Perth, there were only two gay clubs. Para-dice'etcya, was it, in terms of a career in drag. The other, offered rostered spot numbers between a long list of queens.

"Sac, I hate to be the one to tell you this, but better to hear it from me than anyone else. The show is being given to Ima. She put her hand up to carry on with the show once you were rushed to hospital, and I have to say she did really well," said Rudy, informing me of the worst possible scenario *ever.*

"But, she can't. That's *my* show," I said.

"The producers are retitling it as 'Ima in Para-dice', and she will take over as hostess of the production this weekend. I'm sorry."

"No! No, no, no." The conversation was useless, as his hands really were tied, being but the messenger. But the whole situation felt ridiculously unfair. I flashed back to the days of bullying in primary school, and how I was somehow the one that always got the bare end of the stick. As much as I could have begged and pleaded, there was nothing I could have done. My time as hostess and presenter of 'Para-dice with Sacrifice' had ended. My reign as the 'Queen of Para-dice' was over. Being a decent man, Rudy had fought to keep me at the club as a show girl. So, although I was no longer hostess, I became part of the resident line-up of performers. Rudy stated that it would be a position with less responsibility and stress free. I would only need to prepare for my spot numbers, wait to be introduced and, perform.

It certainly was a hard transition for me, having had the spotlight week to week, to all of a sudden stepping down to performing as part of a line-up. However, my name had stuck to the scene, and I still had adoring fans wanting to see my work, regardless of the behind the scenes rumors and bitching. The other queens were friendly to my face, but underneath I knew they were basking in my misfortune.

*

"Hard luck. Who knew Ima would have been the better presenter?" Pablo said one night in the dressing room, walking off to Sharon and Bella, thinking she was hot shit. It was hard to deal with the other queens' attitudes, but I wasn't letting them get the better of me. I loved what I did, drag had become my reason for living, and the feeling I had when I was on

stage was priceless. It really was hard though, as my dream had

unquestionably been squashed. However, in all the time I had been raised, if

there was anything that my mother taught me, it was to be grateful for what

you were given, and I still had my spot as a resident showgirl at Para-dice. I

stayed thankful to Rudy for giving me that.

16 SCENE QUEENS

I now stand across from my dresser, looking into the mirror
dressed in the garment I've chosen to wear for the night, complete with
glittering accessories and, the kitchen knife nestled into my bag. With my
make-up finished, and my hair set to perfection, I look ahead at a queen
who I once upon a time thought was glorious. But tonight, is withered and
faded from a life of consistent torment. I walk through the apartment in
which I now live, on my own as a young adult having given up on men,
with bills stuck to the fridge. Photos of my family are hung on the walls, as
the only remaining part of my life I held any true faith in. The only ones
that had stuck by me. Even Andrew, had drifted from my life. In my garage,
I click the button to open the roller door. As I hear the machinery clink
while the door rises, I get into the driver's seat of the car and place my bag
on the seat beside me. Looking at myself in the rearview mirror, I
remember my shitty life. I wonder how I had been hit so hard and what I

had done to deserve it, or at least why the shit that hit the fan had not flown in the direction of others more deserving. I reversed out of the garage and made my way on to the road. As I drove off, I left behind an apartment full of memories that had more or less become an empty shell to me. I drove motionlessly.

*

Pulling up to the car park behind the club, ahead I see Pablo, Sharon and Bella in their little bandwagon, waltzing their way around to the main street and entrance. All I could ask myself right now was, *where are their spines? What gives them the right to continue life unworried? And why had they drifted through life with such ease?* Sat in my car, it started to rain. Not ready to head inside just yet, I waited, and I flicked the windscreen wipers on. As they waved back and forth, I remember a very recent time I sat here in a similar state, with not a clue of what to do. Perhaps I should have done it then – gotten out of the car and head back inside to end it all. But I couldn't have. What I needed was time, and a plan. Some might ask why I didn't phone the police but, had I done that, some might ask why I let them off so easy. In the end, the police might have dealt with it in a more appropriate manner, but then I wouldn't have had the chance to see them petrified, right before I slit their throats, as justice came spilling out.

Scene Queens, taking the freedom and equality which the generations before us fought so hard and rightfully for, had turned the community into a game of popularity and segregation. Thinking back to what I walked in on, I feel faint, and sick to my stomach. I remember it all so vividly. I'd finished getting ready at home, wearing the same outfit I'm wearing tonight. I stood back and looked into the mirror, though that night I stood proud, making the most of what I had left, standing in my sleek silver sequined gown that fit me like a glove, with my shoulders back and my head held high. I was wearing a stunning crystal necklace my mother and father had given me for my birthday the year I started drag. My hair was pure blonde, pinned up at the back and held up around the sides, sprayed in place with a ringlet either side to frame my face.

That night, the vibe was pumping the minute I walked into the club. The music was loud and the crowd was simply pulsating. As I walked into the dressing room to prepare for my spot, stood by the dresser was the three sheep of the I-squad, while Ima sat drinking a glass of champagne finishing her mascara.

"Eek, did any of you fart? I just got the most awful whiff," said Ima. Sharon, Pablo and Bella looked at me, giggling, and then back at each other as they whispered among one another. I set my costumes for the night on a stand and then made my exit to get a drink. Making my way back out to the club, I walked up to the bar and ordered a gin and tonic. Beside me was a really cute guy with short hair, and clothing which looked like it had spent a little too long in the dryer, with his lower back, belly and hip bones exposed.

"Hey. How are you tonight?" I asked. He looked over at me, confused, with a vacant expression and pupils as large as the moon. He looked about 12 years old, and was off his trolley. He started to drool, just before dropping his head on to the bar. In a state of panic, the bartender went to hand me my drink and I pushed it away as I grabbed the boy. At that moment Absolute approached.

"Girl, is everything all right?" she asked.

"No. Can you please help me? I think we've got an overdose," I said. Absolute reacted with alarm, and we carried the boy through the crowd, through the restricted back corridor and to the club office.

"Thanks, Sacrifice. You don't need this on your shoulders right now. You head back out and let me deal with this," she said.

"Will you be all right?" I asked.

"Babe, it's Para-dice. He's a dime a dozen," she said.

I walked back out to the club, feeling somewhat disorientated. People approached me for photos and I posed emotionless. I had witnessed a boy overdose, rushed off without anyone around us seeming concerned, and the night had carried on as if nothing had happened. The I-squad emerged from the dressing room, and strutted their stuff through the club. They passed by to purposefully bump into me.

"Sorry, girl. Places to be, people in the way," giggled Sharon. Bella looked back at me as the others started to walk away. She looked as if she wanted to apologise on behalf of them, but they all continued to walk on, and so did she. Ima threw her hand into the air.

"Come on, girls!" As they walked off, the music in the club began to overwhelm me, and I felt cornered and claustrophobic among the sea of drunk and drug dosed punters. I made my way to the bathroom, entering the females, as it was drag queen etiquette to do so. As I entered, I ran to the bench and held myself up over a sink. The music was less intense, muffled by the walls. A group of girls came up to me, crowding around, dressed in what my mother would have called a line of belts.

"Hi girl. You okay?" they asked.

"Yeah, fine thanks. Just freshening up," I said, trying to maintain myself.

"Can we get a picture please?" they asked, not really caring how I was feeling. I said they could, knowing once they got their photo they'd be back on the dance floor and out of my space. They took out their phones, and I posed with a forceful expression of enjoyment on my face, then they thanked me and left. Holding myself up over the sink, I looked at into the mirror, seeing an exhausted queen who was close to giving up before me. Assessing what was left, and if I really wanted to be part of it. I decided to go back to the office to check in with Absolute about how I feeling. She'd told me her door was always open, and right now I needed to vent. I'd honestly taken all I could tolerate for the I-squad.

I gathered myself, took a deep breath in and exhaled as I had so many times before. I left the bathroom and headed for the office. As I walked down the narrow corridor, I heard what sounded like laughing and cheering coming from the office. Once I reached the office door, I opened it, walking in to find Ima sat on a chair with her legs crossed, leaning back with her phone pointed ahead. Absolute was mounted on the desk I'd sat with Rudy, with her stockings down by her ankles. She was fucking the boy, the boy I had helped her carry in here, he was sprawled out across the desk – completely lifeless. Sharon, Pablo and Bella stood around them with their costumes off, and their cocks un-tucked, masturbating near the desk.

"What the actual fuck?!" I shouted in disgust, despair and horrific shock. Ima rose her fat arse up from her seat quicker than I'd ever seen her move before, quickly closing the door behind me. Absolute got off from the desk, as the other three parted to gather their garments from around the room. Absolute pulled her stockings up in a rush.

"Sacrifice, sit down. Hear us out," said Absolute.

"Hear you out? Hear you out! You're fucking a fucking passed out kid!" I screamed, as I turned to walk to the door.

"Uh, uh. Sit your butt down," instructed Ima, as she guarded the door. My body tingled, as if all blood-flow had stopped like when your arm goes dead, and my skin soon covered with pins and needles. I walked over to the seat Ima had been sitting, looking at the desk, with the boy lying practically dead. He couldn't have even been eighteen, probably getting in tonight with fake identification. I held my hands to my mouth and started to cry.

"What the fuck is this shit?!" I shouted, ripping off my wig and throwing it onto the floor. I pulled my legs up on to the chair with me, and huddled them. Absolute approached, and knelt beside me, while the others, now partly dressed, looked at each other with concern.

"Get back out there girls. Mingle, mingle!" Absolute shouted. The three girls scampered, and Ima opened the door to let them out, leaving just herself, Absolute and I. "Ima, take the boy. Get him to security and tell them to call an ambulance."

"What the fuck am I meant to say?" asked Ima.

"I don't know. He collapsed on the dance floor, in the bathroom... Use your fucking head!" Absolute shouted. I sat in silence while Ima walked towards the boy, pulled his pants back up and pulled his arms over her shoulders as if piggy-backing a child.

"I don't get paid enough for this shit," said Ima, as she left Absolute and I alone in the room.

"Dime a dozen, hey?" I said.

"What are you getting at, Sacrifice?" Absolute asked.

"I'm getting at the fact that I'm starting to think by the way you're bossing your minions around that this is a regular fucking occurrence!" Absolute looked down at the ground and shook her head, then looked back up at me.

"You love what you do, don't you Sacrifice?" Absolute asked. I glared at her.

"Don't you fucking threaten me!" I said.

"Don't you fucking speak back to me! Babe," she said, standing on her feet and beginning to pace. "All I'm saying is that, with the connections I have, someone might find a kilo of cocaine in your locker tonight. And that it could happen, like that," she said, as she clicked her fingers. "I'm just saying be careful about your actions in these next few hours, or it could be your life on the line."

I was speechless. Absolute let me go. I walked startled out from the office and down the corridor back out to the club. I looked upon the venue, full of punters dancing the night away completely oblivious to the underground activity. At the bar were the I-squad, sipping their drinks from straws. My stomach turned, and I left without even a thought of whether to stay for my performance or not. Back in my car, it started to rain and I turned on my windscreen wipers, watching as they went back and forth. I looked at myself in the rear vision mirror, disgusted that I had not called the police. Tonight, however, I felt glad that I hadn't. If the scene queens were going down, it would be at my hand.

Again, I ask myself, *is it so wrong for me to have gotten into my car tonight with a knife nestled into my bag, entering a venue where I'm not required to show security the interior of my bag as considered royalty? Where I can walk right through the doors off the streets from darkness into a club, filled with bright flashing lights, colour and music, into a room where I'm greeted by adoring fans?*

Is it wrong to get out of the car right now and walk through the crowd of people dancing, to get on the stage and burst my way through the stage door while taking out my kitchen knife to start slitting the throats of every drag queen I see? Or would they be better off left amongst the scene? It's either one of those two options, or serving a wrist slap of a sentence, while I serve time for dealing cocaine. Or should I go down for something *I* actually did, serving time while knowing that what *I* did sought justice and ended any future torment inflicted by them to anyone ever again? *Yes, I think, that's the answer.*

17 THE TRIGGER

The night I arrived home after witnessing the club rape, I felt more and more ill. The, just when I thought I couldn't have been more ill, no sooner than when I walked to my dressing room to put my things away, there was a knock at my front door. I walked back to open it, and there were two policeman on my doorstep.

"Good evening sir… miss," one of the police officers said, uncertain about what to call me. I was still dressed in my sequins, but I was not wearing a wig, with just short messed up hair and smudged make-up from my tears. Glitter covered my face.

"Hello officers," I responded, as my heart began to race, thinking about Absolute's comment about planting cocaine in my locker. My mind began to run twenty billion miles an hour.

"I'm afraid there's been an incident," the second police offer informed me. I stayed silent, wanting to hear what they had to say without implicating anything. "Are your parents' names Marie and Clifford?" My gut dropped, as if off a one hundred stories high of a build.

"Yes," I replied, with a lump forming in my throat.

"And your brother. You had a brother named Luke?" he asked.

"Yes, I *do* have a brother named Luke," I responded.

"Sir, I'm afraid they had an accident, at the residence of..." the officer continued to speak, as my mind began to fuzz. I did not black out.

"Where are they now?" I asked, "Are they in hospital?"

"Sir, did you not hear me? They didn't make it. They're dead," he said, and with those words my mind shut off entirely. "Sir, are you ok sir," their words fuzzed in my mind. I shut the door on them. I turned and rested my back against the door. I looked up to the ceiling with tears streaming out from my eyes as I screamed and clenched my hair, pulling chunks of it out and hitting the door behind me. The tears just kept coming, like a waterfall that never ends. I made my way to the bathroom disorientated, bumping into walls and walking into the door frames. I stood still for a moment, rebalanced myself, and made my way through to the bathroom by the sink. I turned on the tap and began to wash my face. Looking into the mirror, I was a mess. I had made my scalp bleed, pulling on my hair. I stared into the mirror, as I watched blood trickle down my face. I was covered in glitter, blood and tears.

I screamed, over and over. I fell to the floor with the water from the tap continuing to run heavily, and cried myself sleep, curled up on the cold tiles. Waking the next morning, I stood from where I had curled up and slept overnight on the bathroom floor, looking ahead at myself in the mirror. I looked as if I were some kind of zombie. My make-up was in patches, my eyeliner was smudged, my mascara had run and dried down the sides of my face, and my eyebrows and lipstick were worn away. I turned off the tap, which was still running, and made my way to the shower to turn it on. I took off my garments and got inside. I washed off my makeup and scrubbed my face as I began to cry again. Then, for a while, I just let the water run over me.

Completely emotionless, I stepped out the shower and toweled dried my body, then dropped the towel on the floor. I walked to my bedroom and got into bed, placing my phone on the bedside table. Turning my head to face the pillow, I screamed into it. Then, turning to face the bedside table, I reached for my phone and called home. The phone rang and rang, but nobody picked up. I pressed redial over and over again, but each time it was the same. I put the phone down, and closed my eyes, again crying as I drifted to sleep. Unaware of the time, I woke to a phone call. I rubbed my eyes and stretched out, not answering in a rush. Answering it, in a daze, I heard Absolute's voice.

"Girl, where are you? You're on at midnight," she said. "I get that you left last night. But the shows must go on." I rubbed my eyes and held the phone out to see the time, as my eyes focused I saw it was nine o'clock. I had slept all day. "Are you on your way?" asked Absolute.

"I'll be there," I said, hanging up immediately, not caring for her response, with the audacity she had to call me. Then, there I was, sat at my dressing table, surrounded by the large assortment of costumes I had collected over a multitude of years.

Now sat in the car, as I stared at myself in the rear vision mirror, I began to freak out. *Is this really what I want to do? Take a step that I can't take back.* Gathering my thoughts and breathing deep, I started to gain back my determination. My nerves changed to purpose, and my anxiety to decisiveness. I was going to go through with this no matter what the consequences, for all the hell I'd been through at school, at the club, and to make a stand for everyone who had ever been trampled over. But also, because these queens were just darn right evil. The thought of my family now gone, my mum, and that was it, the trigger. I had nothing to lose. All the good in my world had been demolished from my life.

Not phased about the rain, I opened my car door and stepped out. The rain drops hit my wig, fresh makeup and dress with force. I leant in to the backseat of my car, grabbed my bag and shut the door, throwing my keys over my shoulder – I had no more use for them. On I walked, to Para-dice'ecta. As I approached, the bouncers greeted me warmly and lifted their jackets above me so I didn't get wet, even though I was already saturated.

"Evening, Sacrifice. You're soaked. Better get in there and dry up," one of the bouncers said. I looked at him, unresponsive, and continued to walk in as I left them behind. Walking into the club, I looked around, hoping that there was no sight of Ima, hoping that she'd be in the dressing room readying herself to open the night's performances. Ima was nowhere to be seen, and so I continued to walk. I walked with caution, as I couldn't sight the I-squad. Walking up onto the side of stage, I opened the door to the dressing room. I could hear talking inside. Not as I had planned, I walked in to find Ima and Absolute talking with each other.

"You're late!" Absolute stated, as I walked to my locker and placed my bag inside it. My heart began to pound and I started to perspire. *Thankfully I'm drenched, so hopefully they won't notice. All I want is for Absolute to leave so that I can start with Ima. As Absolute's pattern suggests, once she leaves the room she doesn't return until just before show time.* I wanted the whole lot to be finished by then.

"Ima, are you almost done? I need to speak with Sacrifice alone," said

Absolute. I started to fret, trying to keep my cool. Shutting my locker, I walked up to Absolute.

"What can't you say to me in front of Ima?" I asked.

"Never you mind, girl. Patience," she said. I had no idea what to do. I walked back to my locker and opened it. The locker door opened out towards them, and I grabbed the knife from my bag and pushed it down my top between the socks in my bra.

"Ah," I said, letting out a moment of pain. I had jabbed myself in the chest, but only lightly, as I re-adjusted my boobs to hide the handle of the knife. I shut the locker door and looked at Absolute. "Fine then, let's take this to your office," I said.

"Aren't you going to get ready for your show?" asked Absolute.

"Oh, trust me, I'll be ready for my applause when the time comes," I said.

Absolute agreed and told Ima to stay put. *Perfect. Once I get rid of Absolute I can go back for Ima.* Following behind Absolute, I looked around the club at all the unsuspecting punters, completely unaware of what was about to take place. On dancing they would go, right up until the very second I would step back onto that stage to take my final bow before –

being taken away by the authorities. *What a moment it will be. Everyone staring at me in shock while I make my exit in handcuffs, escorted out of the building, smiling with satisfaction while the train of my dress drags behind me, drenched in blood.* Entering the corridor, I watched Absolute walk down it to the office door. I leant my back up against the door to the corridor as I pulled it shut behind me. Absolute opened the office door and looked back at me.

"What are you doing?"

"Just watching" I answered. "Watching the pathetic excuse for a human being you are."

"Right, you're this fucking close to that locker of cocaine, babe! Now get the fuck down here and into my office," she said. I walked slowly, taking in the moment, knowing each step I took brought me closer to slaughtering her.

"*Your* office," I said, as I walked inside and wandered over to the desk where Absolute had fucked the lifeless boy.

"What the hell is up your arse tonight?"

"Not you," I said, smirking as I stared at her. Absolute shut the door and walked closer to me. When she reached me, she tore off my wig and threw it on the ground. I didn't react, in fact I found it slightly amusing.

"Not yet," she said. "I haven't punished you for what you saw the other night," she finished in a sexual tone. I indulged in the behavior for a moment, manipulating her into a vulnerable position.

"Uh, uh, it is *I* that needs to punish you, you bad man," I said, luring her in. Absolute smiled, took off her wig, starting to kiss me. As she did, I quickly reached into my bra, pulled out the knife, and stabbed her in the gut before retracting it. Absolute sprung back and stumbled on her heels, falling to the floor. Hitting the side of her head on the corner of the desk on her way down, blood ran from both her head and stomach. "You were always such a two-faced monster, and I never saw it until the other night. But you always have been, haven't you?" I asked, as I walked up to her, cowering and frightened on the floor as she held her stomach. She was trying to crawl to the door as blood smeared along the floor. She gasped and pleaded for me to let her go. Said, we could call it even. I knelt down on top of her, with my heels either side of her body. I spun her around while her blood dripped from my knife. "And why should I let you go? When that poor boy we brought in here didn't have a choice?"

"He was gone," Absolute murmured, beginning to cough up blood. "He didn't...feel...a thing." She dropped her head to the floor.

"And that's what makes you the worst monster of all," I said, pushing the knife back into her gut one last time. I lifted the knife up and stared at it. Covered in blood, I leant back down and smeared it on her face. *One down, four to go.*

Before leaving the office to make my way back to the dressing room, I kneeled down beside Absolute's decrepit body and laughed with accomplishment. Staring at her, I looked down at her dress and lifted it up, throwing the bulk of it up over her torso and face. A faceless corpse, fit for her spineless being. I got a little closer, and began to pull down her stockings, to her knees. Underneath she had tucked *his* bits away with a special string-pulled type underwear. I cut the string and pulled the underwear away. There was his large flaccid penis. The one I'm sure he would have loved to take to me with. The one I'm sure had taken to many others. I reached down and grabbed it, flopping it from side to side like a piece of raw rump steak, as I contemplated my next move. I then clutched it in my hand, and with my other swiftly started to slice it off. Blood squirted and bled out everywhere. He certainly *had* been hung.

Getting up and leaving the office with Absolute's body sprawled out on the floor, I threw his flaccid floppy penis into a coffee mug which sat on the desk, and walked briskly back into the corridor, shutting the office door closed behind me. I felt vigorous and powerful, as a rush of adrenalin made its way through my body. Before reaching the end of the corridor, I stopped, caught up in the moment, and quickly tucked the knife back into my dress. My hands had become covered in blood, and now so was the front of my dress and bare chest. Conscious of this, I slowly opened the door and looked out. No-one I knew immediately was around, and as such I speedily made my exit and stormed ahead through the dark clusters of punters dancing and drinking, making my way back towards the dressing room.

Once back inside, Ima was applying her mascara – just as I had imagined. Although the room was dimly lit, I was still conscious of my bloody state. *I'll have to do this quick.*

"That was fast," she said, acknowledging me, fancy that. I closed the door behind me.

"And I'll try to make this fast too," I said, walking towards her. As I approached, I took the knife out from my dress. I caught her eyes in the mirror, catching a glimpse of me as I approached. Ima turned around to grab my arm as I went to stab her.

"You crazy bitch," she cried, pushing back on my arms as I pushed forward.

"You're the crazy bitch, Ima! You fucking sicko!" Ima's chair began to tilt, and we both fell to the floor. The knife bounced and slid across the room. Ima struggled as I held her down, reaching for the knife. I kneed her in the crotch and, as she grabbed herself in pain, I got up and ran for the knife, falling back down as I leapt for it and cracked my jaw on the ground coming down. The pain was unbearable, but I soldiered though it, adrenalin taking over as I continued to grab the knife and turned back around to face her.

As I turned, Ima was on her knees and swung at me with one of her heels. It scraped me on the cheek and flew across the room as she fell back down. On the ground, now beside me, I clenched the knife and began to stab her wherever I could. I stabbed and stabbed, as blood gushed out from her body in every direction. As my urgency diminished, I felt a loss of strength in my arms, and collapsed on the floor next to her. I started breathing heavily, and looked to my right where she laid beside me. Where I had been stabbing her was her chest, neck and head – it wasn't a pretty sight. Blood trickled over her eyeballs and neck, down to the floor. I stared at the blood as it dripped to the floor, like droplets of rain from the edge of an umbrella. Regaining my strength, I stood up. My dress was slashed, torn and drenched in blood. I walked to the dresser and placed the knife down on the bench, as my hands slid across it, smearing blood over the countertop.

Seeing myself in the mirror, my jaw was slightly ajar. I slowly tried to open it and smile. Painfully, I managed to clench my teeth, which were also covered in blood. I began to feel a pain in my head. *Not now.* I started inhaling and exhaling deeply as I pressed my hands down on the bench, trying to contain the pain. It slowly faded, just leaving the searing jolts of pain in my jaw. I heard laughter and chatter from outside the door, and then saw the door handle begin to turn. I grabbed the knife and rushed to hide behind the black curtain which lined the walls to the dressing room. *So far so good*, I thought, trying to contain my breathing as I heard the door to the dressing room swing open.

18 A SMIRK

Waiting behind the curtain, I heard the three queens walk in together. How could anyone not recognise those voices? They were so nasally and irritating. They walked in, completely bypassing Ima's body by the lockers on the floor, walking straight to the mirror.

"I heard Harry chooses the boys and then brings them home to Ric," said Bella.

"Ew. Ric and Harry have HIV. Why would anyone sleep with someone if they knew they had HIV?" Sharon asked.

"That's just it, Shazza! They don't know!" said Pablo.

"What do you mean?" asked Sharon.

"Neither Harry or Ric tell the guys," said Pablo.

"That's fucked up," said Bella.

"Not as fucked up as your face," responded Pablo. The trio began to laugh and opened up their makeup cases. I felt sick hearing what Absolute had been up to with her fiancé, Ric. If it was even true, the scene was full of made up rumors and gossip. Regardless, I needed to get this over and done with, someone could find Absolute's body at any moment and have the club shut down. I began to breathe heavily with not much ventilation behind the thick black curtain.

I peered out, looking at the girls sat up at the bench touching up their faces. They still hadn't noticed Ima's body on the floor, which was surprising given the size of her! Pablo even left to go to the toilet, still without noticing. *Fuck, don't go! No! Can't wait any longer! Get this done!* As Pablo left the room, I walked out from behind the curtain directly to Sharon who was closest and, grabbed her head while slitting her throat in one sharp movement. I saw the blood start to gush from her throat in the mirror, then her body fell to the floor, and Bella turned to stare in shock. I thought she would have run, but she didn't. She always was the quieter one. I laughed, and then coughed in pain with the taste of blood in my mouth.

"Hi," I said, grinning.

"Fuck, Sacrifice. What the hell happened to you?" asked Bella.

"To me? What the fuck happened to *me*? I'm fine. I'm just cleaning up the mess around here," I said.

"I agree, things have gotten pretty messy, but you've gone fucking psycho, girl," she said, holding her hands up to try and calm me.

"Maybe," I said, grabbing a large make-up case by its handle from the bench and slamming it over her head. I cackled evilly, as she fell to the floor. I felt so mighty and all-powerful. Never had I felt such exhilaration. This beat virginity any day.

"Three down, two to go," I said to myself as I knelt down to where Bella struggled on the floor, holding her head.

"Sacrifice, you don't have to do this," Bella said, struggling to speak. "You've always been a good person. What will people think of you?" I hummed Barbra's 'Here's to Life', while stroking Bella's hair.

"The ones who mattered to me are gone, and I really couldn't give a flying fuck what the rest think," I said, struggling to speak myself, as the pain in my jaw persisted and drool mixed with my blood. As I placed the knife underneath her neck, I moved my fingers underneath her wig, and yanked her head back by her real hair. She started to cry out loud.

"I'm so sorry!" Bella screamed. I stared at her for a moment longer.

"For not including you, for just standing by, for being so self-indulgent.

The truth is, I've always had a bit of a crush on you, Michael," she said. I

shook my head in confusion and shut my eyes. I looked back at her and

pressed the knife up against her neck, slitting it wide open. I got a bit teary

for a moment, but what was I supposed to do? She had become a witness,

and if I stopped now I wouldn't have got to finish what I started. Gathering

my strength, I stood back up and walked over to the side of the door,

waiting for Pablo to return. Staring at the dead queens and blood that now

saturated the floor – I was rather proud of my work.

*

As Pablo walked back in, I pushed her from behind so she fell onto

the floor with what was now almost a pool of blood. I slammed the door

shut, locking it from inside. Pablo tried to get up, slipping on the blood and

fell back. She screamed, shouting that I was a fucking bitch and that she'd

rolled her ankle. I walked over to her and knelt down beside her, leaning on

one knee. She looked at me with true fright in her eyes.

"So this is it, then?" she asked. I just stared, taking in my final victim.

She began to laugh. I tried to resist the pain in my jaw, asking what was so

funny. "Ranga, ranga, ranga," she began to chant, as she laughed in

hysterics. I took off her wig, revealing blonde hair. I had never seen Pablo

as a boy, but now looking at him in drag saw recognisable features hidden underneath the masking of contour.

"You!" I screamed in agony, as my jaw cracked. I stabbed her in the side of the arm, like the day I'd stabbed her with a pencil as a school boy. "You made my life hell!" I forced out, becoming numb to the pain. I withdrew the blade from her arm, raising it in the air above my head, to hold it with both hands. I began stabbing her repeatedly. Blood squirted out onto my face each time the blade entered her chest, and my hands dripped with blood. I dropped the knife and fell to the floor, not feeling as amazing as I had hoped when I finished. Rolling on to my side, I looked at the bodies around me, like a toybox of pretty dolls. I'd always liked playing with dolls as a child. I placed my hand down in front of my face, in a puddle of blood, rubbing it to feel its warmth. But it was now cold. Suddenly, I didn't feel so powerful. I came down, *hard*. My mind began to fuzz in and out.

Gathering my strength, I pushed myself up from the ground, with thick strings of blood beginning to coagulate which stuck to me. I stood, with blood dripping from my head, my jaw, my hands and my dress. My mind continued to fuzz in and out, with my vision beginning to blur. My head felt as though it was truly about to explode. Walking over to the mirror, I stood and stared at what I had become. I looked at myself, fuzzing and blurring in and out of my mind and sight. I turned back around and leant down to pick up the knife, turning back to face the mirror. I looked down at my wrist, circling the knife around it, as I had done in primary school. I screamed an almighty scream as surging pain pierced through the front of my head. Then, there was a knock at the door.

"Hello, hello! It's that time of the month Ric comes out to play!" I stood, seconds away from slitting my wrists to end the pain, but something prevented me from doing so.

"Sorry, who is it?" I called out. Holding my jaw and head, in scrutinising agony, while I approached the door.

"It's Ric! Harry's fiancé! I've got her music for tonight!"

"Give me two seconds." I looked back to the mirror, with my vision starting to clear, seemingly hallucinating, as Mrs Cornel from Lumiere popped up beside me, as she placed her hand on my shoulder. A purple glow filled the dressing room.

"Throughout history, it has been the inaction of those who could have acted that has made it possible for evil to triumph," she said.

Looking down at the knife held in my hand, and back up to the mirror, I formed a smirk. Though Ric, hadn't been part of the plan, I did still need to take my final bow. With the slightest bit of adrenalin and feeling of purpose returning to my body, I turned around to the door.

Looking down at the handle, I grabbed it and turned it, opening the door.

As I swung the door open, I looked ahead to see Ric's face, mortified at the

sight of me. *Oh, how I'm just as mortified, Mr. Transmitter.* Before he had a

chance to react, I grabbed his shirt from the neckline and pulled him in

towards me, as my other hand forced the knife into his throat. I let go of

the handle and pushed him back with the knife still wedged in his throat. As

he fell, his face was vacant of expression. His body hit the stage floor, and

as it did, my head began to pulse. I stumbled out over his body, towards

center stage, while holding my forehead in pain. I steadied myself, looking

down at Ric as blood trickled from his throat. Finally, with my last ounce of

strength, I used the muscles in my neck to lift my head and look out to the

club. My vision began to re-blur, but even with impaired vision, I could

make out that all eyes were on me. Every face in the club, was looking my

way, as if they had seen a ghost – instead it was a blood drenched drag

queen. The music had cut. My head felt heavy. Trying to take a step

forward, my foot caught the front of my bloody dress. Unbalanced and off

guard, with one final breath, I lunged back and fell forward. My final bow

on stage. Fuzz, and then Blackness.

Printed in Great Britain
by Amazon

12897245R00155